I0557606

# Nanna

*A Novel*

*Sequel to 'Joy came in the Morning'*

## Yema Lucilda Hunter

# Nanna

ISBN: 978-99910-54-25-4

**Sierra Leonean Writers Series**

c/o Mallam O. & J. Enterprises
120 Kissy Road, Freetown; Warima, Sierra Leone
Publisher: Prof. Osman Sankoh (Mallam O.)
publisher@sl-writers-series.org

# DEDICATION

In loving memory of the quintessential 'Nanna', my
godmother,
Lady Mary Bankole-Jones

More things are wrought by prayer than this world
dreams of.

*Alfred Lord Tennyson*

# ACKNOWLEDGEMENT

I won't name names this time, but do appreciate the support I received from friends and family who took the time to read the manuscript at different stages of its development and then gave me useful feedback, or provided me with information I needed for certain sections. God bless you all.

# PROLOGUE

Each time Cobola Ennison had to go into Freetown, she grumbled about how long it took to travel a mere six miles. As usual, she was alone in the taxi, but by the time they reached Ascension Town Cemetery, the oppressive heat, petrol fumes and black smoke belching from beat-up lorries, had brought on a headache. She took a deep, slow breath before heading for the grave she had come to visit. It lay beyond two towering silk cotton trees, some distance away from the road that ran through the cemetery. She was so pleased that the City Council now controlled grass that had flourished unchecked during the Rebel War and its immediate aftermath. This made it less likely that she would twist her arthritic ankle on the concealed concrete edges of graves; but, even so, it wasn't easy to reach her destination.

Once there, she spent a few moments looking down at the marble tombstone whose inscription read:

**KWEKU DANIEL ENNISON**
**October 1, 1931 – November 14, 1991**
**A devoted husband and father**
**†**
**Dearly loved. Sadly missed**
**RIP**

Apart from visits on New Year's Day and on the anniversary of his death, Cobola still went to the cemetery to inform her late husband of every significant event in her life. On this occasion, she had come to tell him that she'd just returned from America.

'You would have enjoyed it-o,' she said as she picked off the dead leaves littering the whitewashed concrete surface of the grave. 'It's a *wonderful* country.'

So much had happened in the years since she had placed that tombstone. In addition to identical twins, Eric and Derek, babies when Kweku died, her son, Yao and his wife, Isabella, had produced a daughter. Cobola had been quite annoyed that they named her Adora, after Kweku's mother, but she'd hidden her vexation and soon recovered. Of far greater importance had been her marvelous reunion with the son she had had to give up for adoption in the 1950s. He was now an American eye specialist called Orlando West, and had visited Sierra Leone the previous year to see how he could help pick up the pieces in his birthplace which, from all accounts, had been shattered by conflict. It was in the course of his investigations that he had met Isabella, Yao, and subsequently, Cobola herself. Cobola had discovered that Orlando had a family of his own – a wife, Beverly, also an eye specialist, two sons, a daughter-in-law, and a granddaughter. The trip to America had been to meet them all.

Every time she went to the cemetery, Pa Cowan, the wiry little man she paid a small annuity to tend Kweku's grave, somehow got wind of her arrival – even when there were no other workers visible. As usual, he came running up in his sweat-stained singlet and ragged khaki shorts to assure her, with his bad stammer, that he was doing the work, 'All the time, ma; all the time'. Cobola smiled, knowing what was expected of her.

'So I see,' she said, and fished in her bag for a ten thousand leone note. 'The grave is looking nice, and the flowers we planted are doing well.'

Certain now of his supply of local gin for the rest of the day, Pa Cowan's stammer accompanied her cheerfully to where Alimamy was waiting beside his car.

Alimamy was Cobola's favourite among the three taxi drivers she had listed on her mobile phone. He was almost never late for appointments and always willing to do small errands that saved her from having to get out of the car along the way. Furthermore, she never had to ask Alimamy to turn down his music or put out a cigarette. And he was always ready to offer an opinion on the events of the day which led to some interesting conversations.

Driving into the city with him was the only thing that made it bearable to be stuck in traffic.

'Take me to Wilkinson Road, ya,' she said. 'I have to see Mrs. Kargbo.'

Fifteen minutes later, Alimamy placed a large plastic bag beside the front door of the bungalow where Cobola's oldest friend, Gertrude, lived with her husband, Abu. It was full of the gifts Cobola had brought them from the States.

'When shall I come, ma?'

'In two hours,' she told Alimamy, and announced her presence.

The women had been chatting for a while when Cobola said,

'Trudy, life is strange, eh? Had it not been for that stupid war, and had Bella not been working for that NGO, *Health for the World*, I would never have seen my first-born again, I would never have known that I had other grandchildren, and a great-grandchild, and I know for sure that I would never have gone to America.'

Gertrude's response was to lean forward, open her eyes wide and sing in her deep and husky voice,

*'God moves in a mysterious way…'*

Cobola had never been able to carry a tune, but she still sang along with Gertrude: *'his wonders to perform. He plants his footsteps in the sea and drives away the storm…'*

They were chuckling over this rather irreverent rendition of one of Freetown's favourite hymns when Sia, Gertrude's house help, brought in a tray with glasses of iced ginger beer and a saucer piled high with freshly made rice *akara,* and pepper sauce. Gertrude licked her lips in anticipation of pleasure.

'Cobs, come let us enjoy,' she said. 'Nice food is the only thing that takes me close to heaven these days.'

After more than sixty years of friendship, Cobola was so used to Gertrude's earthy humour, that she merely said,

'As for you!'

'Am I lying?' Gertrude retorted as they settled down to eat.

'No, but only you would say it.'

With a chuckle as throaty as her voice, Gertrude dipped one of the fried balls made with rice flour and banana in the pepper sauce.

'So gist me about America,' she said.

'*Gist?* What is that now – a new slang? '

Gertrude let out another chuckle.

'It's what young Nigerians say when they want their friends to share gossip or tell them the latest news…Nigerian films are all the rage now-o.'

'Ehn,' Cobola said. She wasn't at all familiar with Nigerian films. In fact, what with the lack of electricity in George Town, she hadn't watched television since the time the rebels attacked Freetown and its environs and she had been forced her to spend a month with Yao, who had a generator. She washed down the *akara* with ginger beer and exhaled gustily before saying, with a shake of her head,

"Trudy, Sierra Leone is far behind-o – far, far behind. First of all, let me tell you about Accra.'

She had undertaken the journey to visit Orlando and his family with a good deal of anxiety, made worse when she realised that she would have two days to wait in Accra for a Delta Airlines flight that would take her straight to Atlanta, Georgia. Yao offered to accompany her to Accra, and they had stayed at a guest house close to the vast complex of buildings that make up the Korle Bu Teaching Hospital. The reservation had been made for a Yao Ennison and, assuming he was Ghanaian with that name, the owner, a friendly man called Nii Areyeetey, had automatically welcomed them in Asante Twi, which was the local lingua franca. Yao explained that he had a blood connection with Ghana, through his grandfather, but didn't know any Ghanaian language; to which Nii Areyeetey replied in his jovial way, 'Never mind, you are still a brother,' and offered to show them something of the city while running errands the next day. Cobola now said to Gertrude,

'In the parts he showed us, there were traffic lights everywhere, and most of them were working. And there were policemen on motor-bikes controlling traffic at busy intersections, not just making way for presidential motorcades. They have roads on top of roads – they call them flyovers, and some wide, wide streets with plenty of shade trees. And everything so *clean*. You should see the area around their Black Star monument and parade grounds, and the marble structure they have built for Kwame Nkrumah's tomb! Impressive-o. Even when the plane was descending the night before, I could hardly believe my eyes. The lights were like a carpet of stars below us…Trudy, to tell you the truth, I felt ashamed of our backwardness…'

Over the years, Cobola had learned that there was no one more loyal than Gertrude Kargbo, whether it was to her friends, her family or her country. She was therefore not at all surprised when Gertrude pursed her lips and eyed her with disapproval.

'Cobs, I'm sure that man only took you to the best parts of Accra,' she said. 'And don't forget it's not long since *we* came out of a war.'

'I haven't forgotten, Trudy, but still…And why did we have to have a war in the first place? Anyway, that was Accra. Yao saw me off the next evening. I had dosed myself well, so my arthritis had gone to hide; but Yao still arranged a wheel chair for me as Orlando had suggested…Trudy, you should have seen that plane! It was as high as a storey building. When I thought about its own weight, so many passengers, all that cargo, and flying non-stop for more than ten hours, I remembered what people used to say in the colonial days: that the white man is next to God.'

'Some people still believe that,' Gertrude interjected.

'Not the young ones-o,' Cobola said, and continued her story.

'Except for the noise of the engine, it wasn't even as if we were moving. Not like that small plane that took me to Banjul after Kweku's funeral and nearly gave me a heart attack… Orlando had told me that I should move around to avoid getting blood clots in my legs, so I went up and down the aisle between the seats a few times – even when I didn't feel like going to the toilet…'

'You are lucky to have a son who is a doctor,' Gertrude said. 'How many people know an important thing like that? By the way, how are they getting on in Bo?'

'They say they like the town, and that the government officials they have seen are very happy about their plans to provide a free eye clinic for one month every year. The town council has already given them a building to use...'

'*Enh*. That's good-o!'

'Yes, I'm praying that it works out so I can look forward to seeing Orlando every year...Where was I?'

'You went up and down to the toilet so you wouldn't get blood clots in your legs...'

'Oh, yes,' Cobola said, biting into another *akara*. 'When we got to Atlanta, they announced that everyone who needed assistance should remain seated. My foot was still okay, but by then I was fagged out and my ears were blocked, so I didn't move one inch till a young black man came to get me. His hair was cornrowed...'

'You mean like a woman?' Gertrude asked in disbelief.

'Just like a woman; he had made a style and all. And that was nothing,' Cobola went on. 'You should see what some of them do with their hair, especially the young ones. Some have long, long *dada* like that Bob Marley – they call it dreadlocks. Some of the ones with short hair let the barbers make designs on their heads – circles, triangles, zigzag lines…Anyway, this boy took me to a special immigration queue for people in wheel chairs, helped me to get my suitcase, and handed me over to Orlando and his wife. He was nice-o. He even tried to make conversation while we were waiting; but with my tiredness and blocked ears, his American twang was too much for me. I could hardly understand him, except when he asked where I came from. I answered, 'Sierra Leone' and he said, 'South America?' After that I just gave him sweet smiles when he spoke to me. He must have thought I was stupid… Orlando's house isn't very far from the airport, but I couldn't keep my eyes open when I sat in his car…'

'I hope your mouth wasn't gaping,' Gertrude said. She dropped a whole *akara* into hers and smothered another in sauce.

'Even if it was, they wouldn't have noticed. I was in the back seat.'

'Orlando would have seen you through his driving mirror; anyway, tell me about their house; and you know *I* like details…'

'Let me drink first. This ginger beer tastes almost as good as what my mother-in-law used to make. May she rest in peace.'

Cobola's pious wish sounded somewhat insincere, as well it might. Kweku's mother hadn't wanted her to marry her son and they never became friends though, for his sake, they had treated each other with courtesy. Knowing the whole story, Gertrude added an 'Ay-men' in a similar tone of voice.

'Orlando's house is on one floor like yours, but with a green lawn all round it like a carpet,' Cobola continued, 'And it has five bedrooms. Their own, and the one they gave me, have private bathrooms and toilets. In their bathroom, there is one sink for Orlando and one for his wife…'

Gertrude's mouth fell open, exposing remnants of the *akara* she was chewing.

'You don't mean it!'

'It's true. His and hers,' Cobola answered with emphasis. 'And the house has nice wooden floors with beautiful carpets, except in the kitchen. Even the bathrooms and toilets have carpets – small ones, but thick. They have four freezers, and one big air-conditioner that makes the whole house comfortable no matter how hot it is outside. Those are in the cellar, which is not like any cellar I had seen before. They call it their basement. Part of it is like another small parlour. That is where Orlando listens to his music. And you should see their television, Trudy – three times the size of yours! They keep it locked in a cabinet, so when no one is watching, you won't even know it's there. And their garage can take two big cars.'

'*Hey!* And *they* are just ordinary people.'

'Not so ordinary-o. Don't forget that both of them are doctors. Doctors make money in America, and Orlando and his wife are specialists.'

'Beverly, right? Is she nice?'

'Yes, Beverly. Very nice. She calls everybody 'honey', not only Orlando and their children...I have a feeling she's older than him. Her hair is grey.'

'You can't go by that-o; don't forget Orlando shaves his head.'

'Something tells me she is older,' Cobola insisted.

'And the grandchildren; did they take to you?'

Cobola's expression grew tender.

'Trudy, it's as if God is trying to make up for allowing that lorry to kill Kweku. Orlando's children accepted me as if they had known me all their lives, particularly the older one who is married – Ronald. He said I was their only grandparent still alive and asked if they could call me, Nanna. As for his daughter, Keisha, even Yao's Adora wasn't as cute at that age. And the wife is expecting again. *She's* called Wendy, and she likes to *cook* – just like Bella. I spent a nice weekend with them before going to Washington D.C. to visit George and Tina Tucker –

Bella's parents. You remember that Bella's big sister, Lillian, sponsored them to go to America during the Rebel War. Well, I don't think *they* are ever coming back. Lily is divorced now, so there's no son-in-law in the house to make them feel unwelcome. Tina helps Lily to cook and look after the children, and George has got a part-time job in a supermarket.'

'*Ehn*!' Gertrude said. 'What about you, Cobs? If Orlando invites you to stay with them won't you like to live in America? Water and electricity every day, two doctors in the house?'

'And leave all of you here? *Never*, even though half the time I was lost in wonder, love and praise. Those skyscrapers I so wanted to see? Amazing. Also the size and quantity of everything. They have roads that can take six lanes of traffic going one way, and big, big shops, *full* of things. As for the food, Trudy, the *food*! Those people *eat-o*! You think you are fat? You have to go to America to see huge people – men as well as women. Unbelievable! But I also saw poor-looking people, really, really poor, especially among the blacks. Some of them looked as if their hair hadn't felt a comb for years. And you should have seen their dirty feet and shabby clothes, Trudy! Sad-o, in that rich country. Beverly said some of them have nowhere to go; they live in the street. And that many of them are drug addicts or drunkards.' Cobola chortled unexpectedly. 'She called them 'dranks'. At first I thought it was their word for drunkards, then I realised that she was saying 'drunks'. It was her twang that made it sound like 'dranks'.'

She paused to savour the last of her *akara* and clean her fingers before telling Gertrude, who was still chuckling over 'dranks', 'I'm happy I had the opportunity to see America and the rest of my family-o, but to tell the truth, I wasn't sorry when it was time to come home – no neighbours to talk to, nobody passing in the street, no cocks crowing in the morning...When my people were at work, it was just me, the television, magazines, and the microwave – Monday to Friday, till Orlando showed me how to use his computer and this wonderful thing they call the internet. I was able to get any information I wanted, and I enjoyed that, but I couldn't do it for long. My *eyes*...America is a wonderful place to visit-o, but to live there? Permanently? Maybe, for young people looking for a better life; not for an old cow like me... Here. Let me give you your presents...The dress, the slippers, the cream, and the nightie are for you. The shirts are for Abu...Where is he, by the way?'

Gertrude sucked her teeth,

'As for that one,' she said, 'he doesn't know he should rest more with his diabetes. He still goes to meet his *kabudu* almost every day after breakfast – those of them that are still alive. They drink palm wine and talk their idle talk. He'll come home when he starts feeling hungry...'

In spite of her dismissive attitude, Cobola knew that Gertrude was fond of her husband, though, unlike hers with Kweku, their relationship had never been what anyone would describe as romantic. She said, 'The other things are for the rest of the house... *You* will decide who gets what.'

Gertrude was still admiring the gifts and lavishing Cobola with praise, when Alimamy knocked on the frame of the front door which had been left open to catch the breeze. He saluted smartly from the doorway.

'Yes, ma.'

'I'm coming right now,' Cobola answered.

' Cobs, I'm glad you are back-o,' Gertrude said as they parted. 'Six months without your company was just too long,'

'Six months without yours was too long for me too. If I ever go back to America, it won't be for that long. Home is home, ya – especially at our age.'

# ONE

Not long after Cobola returned from the States, pressure began to mount for her to leave George Town and move in with Yao and his family. She was certain Orlando had a hand in it because while she was there he had said, albeit in his mild way,

'M.A., that house of yours is not suitable for a person your age, particularly when you have a condition that's making your feet unstable. We'd all be much happier if you were to move in with Yao.'

Cobola gave him her sweetest smile and promised to think about it. But she had no intention of doing so, being too certain that, as had happened when she stayed with the younger Ennisons before, she would find it hard to endure Isabella's bossiness and what she considered Yao's excessive docility. Discussing the situation with Gertrude at the time, she had said, 'Trudy, I brought up Yao to respect women and be a gentleman; but where Bella is concerned, he is too much. That girl wears the trousers in their house. It gets on my *nerves*.'

Gertrude had said, 'Cobs, it's *their* life. Mind your own business.'

So far, Cobola had succeeded in keeping her opinion to herself, but she still wished Yao would assert himself more, and wondered whether she could contain her irritation if she lived with them permanently, even if it was in the larger house he was talking of building on land left to him by her father's sister.

One Saturday morning, he turned up to show her the plans.

'And where is the money coming from when you have three children to educate?' Cobola asked at once.

'M.A., don't let that worry you,' Yao answered soothingly. 'For the last ten years we've been saving most of Bella's salary – ever since she left the civil service and started working for *Health for the World;* and my Managing Director has agreed for the company to guarantee a bank loan for me. When we move, we'll rent the top floor of our present house. With what you are getting for the ground floor, we'll have enough to feed us. We just have to pray for good health... Come and see.'

He spread out on her table a blueprint for a sprawling, yet modest, H-shaped bungalow.

'Look. This is your own section here...' he said, with a grin that revealed the dimple he had inherited from his father. 'You see? We won't be in each other's way at all, if that's what is worrying you. You even have your own front door, your own small kitchen, bathroom, sitting-room and veranda, as well as a room for Ida. You can be as independent and as private as you like. The only direct connection from our place to yours will be along this corridor here, and through this door – just for convenience…'

'Looks like it will be very nice, Yao,' Cobola said.

'So you'll come?'

That day, Cobola almost agreed to leave George Town. For her, Freetown's lovely seascapes had always been the city's greatest charm, and the view from Yao's house, which would be off the Barracks Road in the Murray Town suburb, would span White Man's Bay, the King Tom peninsula, and beyond. Besides, she would have access to electricity and running water, since Yao already had a generator and planned to sink a well with a pump; *and* she would be closer to her grandchildren of whom she saw much too little. There was the added advantage of the closeness of Murray Town to the top part of Wilkinson Road, which meant that Gertrude's house would be almost within walking distance. Nevertheless, all she did was to clasp Yao by the arms and say,

'Thanks for the invitation, my dear. It's very sweet of you and Bella; but let me stay where I am for now.'

Yao built the house just as he planned it, hoping that his mother would change her mind by the time it was completed Cobola, however, remained adamant in her refusal to budge.

During that period, anyone asking her about her life would have received the answer she often gave before her reunion with Orlando: 'I'm just living, my dear.' The absence of her beloved Kweku made her daily existence a reflection of the thought conveyed in a sombre wedding hymn much loved by the people of Freetown. The last verse begins: *And when the day shall come when death must part them, one standing lonely,* and goes on in that tear-jerking vein. Years earlier, when she was still in her early sixties, Gertrude had tried to interest her in one of Abu's friends, saying in typical fashion, 'Cobs, just to keep you juicy.' Cobola had answered, 'Juicy for what? Trudy, Let me be…ya? When you've had the best, you can forget the rest.' Not that she was depressed; she was just lacking in joie de vivre. If she felt up to it, she attended meetings of the Mothers' Union, and went to Early Communion at St. George's Cathedral on Wednesday mornings. She avoided choral services as far as possible because the choir still reminded her too poignantly of Kweku: his velvety voice, how fine he looked in his cassock and surplice, and his little wink if their eyes met when he was processing down the aisle. She exchanged regular visits with Gertrude, read as much as her eyes would allow and did her canvas embroidery while listening to the radio. On Sundays, Yao visited her with his family after church, and now and again, her former neighbour, Manny Martin, dropped in, with or without his wife, Hamida. Apart from family occasions and the odd funeral vigil or laying-out, that was the extent of her social life. Only another, much shorter, trip to America and the Wests' annual visit to run their eye clinic lifted her existence above the humdrum.

Two days after her seventy-sixth birthday, she tripped and fell while making her way down the back stairs to the toilet. Searing pain shot through her left arm, and she screamed. Her helper, Ida, was gathering oranges at the time and, having rushed to see what had happened, had the presence of mind to call a neighbour to help her take Cobola into the house and onto her bed. Almost certain that her left forearm was fractured, Cobola sank down on her pillow, muttering, 'Father, thank you that it wasn't my leg or my hip'. Then she asked Ida to pass her mobile phone.

So seldom did she call Yao at work that she almost managed a smile, imagining his concerned frown when he saw her number.

'M.A., has something happened?'

'I fell down the steps...'

'Oh, no!' Yao exclaimed before she could go on, 'Hush, ya? Are you hurt?'

'I think my arm is broken...'

Cobola realised she sounded tearful and hated herself for it, knowing that, as he had been doing for the last two years, Yao would seize this fresh opportunity to raise the matter of her moving over to his house.

'But you are otherwise okay?'

'I think so; it's just the pain. It's *terrible...*'

'Hold on; I'm coming.'

Some hours later, with her left forearm in a cast, and her agony eased by an injection, they were on their way back to George Town. Cobola had once again firmly rejected the idea of moving to Yao's house, even temporarily, since tests had shown that her fall hadn't been caused by a stroke – one of her secret fears once she entered her seventies. Yao was making no attempt to hide his irritation at having to drive east during the evening rush hour. Many of the thousands of people from the provinces, who fled to Freetown during the Rebel War had stayed on, and now lived in the eastern suburbs, swelling the normal population. At this time of day, everyone was heading home either on foot, crammed in taxis, in the dilapidated mini-buses called *poda-podas*, or else riding one of the scores of motorcycle taxis known as *okadas*. *Okada* drivers seemed to disobey traffic rules with impunity, hence the widespread rumour that they were owned by policemen. They overtook on the left and right, emerged from junctions and intersections at will, and scooted in and out of gaps in the traffic as if possessed of a death wish. One of them suddenly cut in front of Yao. He was about to yell the most vulgar curse word he knew, when he remembered that his mother was sitting beside him and swallowed the obscenity. Having to do that increased his annoyance, and he said with unusual impatience,

'M.A., you shouldn't be living so far away from us, and in that dangerous house. You are just being stubborn.'

'As if I couldn't have fallen down at your place,' Cobola retorted.

'Yes, but we don't have steps...Our house won't be so risky for you.'

'Ida is there; I can cope,' Cobola said in a tone that closed the subject.

However, the outpouring of concern and sympathy that came by way of phone calls from Isabella, the twins, Adora, Gertrude, and then Yao again, began to weaken her resolve. By the time, Orlando, Beverly, and her other grandchildren called from the States, she was barely managing to stand her ground; but she continued to do so till Yao phoned her in the middle of the afternoon about two months later. Her fracture had healed by then, though she was still going into town every week for physiotherapy.

'M.A., I need to see you,' Yao said. 'Expect me by six o'clock.'

It was so unusual for him to visit her during the week that Cobola knew at once that something must be wrong. While waiting for him, she not only sent up a prayer, but also took deep, slow breaths, following advice she had read in one of Beverly's magazines when she was in the States.

One look at Yao's bleak eyes and turned down mouth was enough to tell her that her anxiety was justified. He gave her a quick kiss, sat down and got straight to the point.

'M.A., Bella has a lump in her breast… '

'Jesus!' Cobola said, gripping both arms of her chair as her heart lurched. 'Where is she now?'

'Probably at home. One of their official cars usually drops her off.'

'Call her. I want to say something.'

Yao clicked on a number and handed his mother the mobile phone. The moment Isabella answered, Cobola said with no preliminary greeting,

'Bella. You believe in God, don't you?'

'Yes, M.A., I believe in God,' Isabella said, her voice subdued. 'So Yao has told you.'

'Yes, my dear, Yao has told me. Listen. From now on, I want you to keep your mind on God, you hear me? Not on this problem – on God.'

'Yes, M.A.'

'I'll talk to you later. Just hold on to the thought of God's goodness and mercy…ya?'

'Yes, M.A. Thank you.'

As she handed back the phone, Cobola gave Yao a stern look.

'And you, too, you hear?'

'Yes, M.A.'

'Alright; tell me more.'

'The doctor says the lump is suspicious and has to be removed at once and examined…The thing is, if we have it removed here, they'll have to send the specimen to Ghana or South Africa. We don't want to waste time, so I'm taking Bella to Accra on Sunday. I've already phoned Areyeetey to book a room in his guest house, and her doctor has contacted an oncologist at Korle Bu Hospital…We have an appointment first thing on Monday morning…'

'And you want me to keep an eye on the house while you are away. Is that it?'

'Yes, M.A. Please. Khadi, is very reliable, but she's off every weekend till Sunday evening so she can spend some time with her son. He lives with her sister at King Tom to be near his school. Also, we

9

don't trust her to be firm with the children. She tends to let them have their own way.'

Cobola chuckled.

'And you think *I* won't, eh?'

'I know you won't. I haven't forgotten how strict you were with me. Pops was always the soft one, except for that one time he slapped my face for giving you back talk over cleaning my room... Remember?'

'How could I forget? Your father hardly ever lost his temper, but when he did, sparks flew.'

'I miss him, you know,' Yao said after a pause. 'Often.'

'With me it's still every day,' Cobola answered sadly. Before Yao's tender expression could make her start feeling sorry for herself, she tapped his knee.

'Back to business.'

'So can I come for you on Saturday?'

'Of course; and I'll go with Ida. We'll just lock up this house. Nothing worth stealing here, anyway.'

'Thank you, M.A. I have hired a driver to take Adora to and from school. He's called Sheku Tarawallie. You can use him whenever you want to... The boys can fend for themselves since their own school is just down the road...What else? What else? What else?' he muttered, rubbing a hand over his head which, to Cobola's regret, was now as clean-shaven and shiny as his brother Orlando's. She said,

'A hug, my dear. You look as if you need a hug. Come here let me give you one.'

Yao held her tightly when she wrapped her arms around him.

'M.A., I'm scared-o,' he said. 'Really scared.'

Cobola was more than a little frightened herself, but being a strong believer in the benefits of affirming one's faith, she said with the utmost conviction,

'Yao, God is good. Don't ever forget that.'

# TWO

It was her granddaughter, Adora, who started chipping away at her resistance to moving permanently to Murray Town. On the night of her parents' departure for Accra, Adora asked if she could sleep in Cobola's bed.

'Alright, darling,' Cobola said, but no talking-o. I like to be quiet when I've said my prayers.

Adora promised, but then Cobola heard her sniffing away tears and drew her close.

'Mummy will be alright, you hear?'

Not being sure what the parents had told them, she merely repeated, 'She'll be alright.'

'But why did Daddy have to take her all the way to Ghana?' Adora asked. 'There are doctors and hospitals here.'

'Your mother needs special tests and they don't have the machines to do them here, that's all. She'll be alright.'

That answer seemed to satisfy Adora and she soon fell asleep. Cobola had long forgotten what it was like to have another person lying next to her. That night, she found as much comfort in the warmth of Adora's slight body as Adora seemed to find in hers.

The following morning, she was discussing the day's meals with the house help, Khadi, when the twins appeared for breakfast.

'Good morning, Grandma,' they said. Their identical grins and perfect teeth were always endearing reminders of their grandfather's radiant smile, but when Cobola noticed their trousers hanging well below their waists, she folded her arms under her breasts and eyed them with disapproval.

'And where do you think you are going dressed like that?'

'Gramma, that's how most of them dress now-o,' Khadi cut in before the boys could answer.

'I'm very surprised your parents and your school allow it.'

'I don't know about the school, ma, but Daddy and Mummy don't allow it,' Khadi informed her, unasked.

'So you wanted to try it with me, eh?' Cobola said. 'Go straight back to your room.'

She shooed them away, saying to their departing backs. 'Don't let me see you here again till you are properly dressed, you hear me?'

Eric and Derek exchanged sheepish grins and did as they were told.

'What is this country coming to?' Cobola said.

13

She had posed the question aloud, but didn't expect an answer. Khadi , however, compressed her lips to show her own poor opinion of the present state of affairs.

'Gramma, that is all the children think about now-o – fashion.'

Determined to discourage what she considered Khadi's overfamiliarity, Cobola ignored the remark and, though she continued to speak, lowered her voice as if she were having a private grumble. 'It just goes to show how the street can spoil children – even those from decent homes…And the thing is, they look so foolish…'

'Yes, ma. Like scarecrows – as if the trousers don't belong to them.'

Since Khadi had obviously failed to get the message, Cobola pursed her lips and, without another word, went to see what was keeping Adora.

She got on well with the boys though, once, having taken her measure, they realised that their grandmother wasn't a pushover. To her delight, she discovered that with the passage of time, they'd lost their former dislike of physical expressions of affection and kissed her voluntarily when they came in from school. They made recommendations about which shows to watch on the television, and taught her how to use the remote control to find channels with soap operas, Nigerian movies and church services. They also taught her how to send text messages on her mobile phone – all that without ever making her feel that they were obeying parental instructions to 'look after Grandma'. By the time she had been with them a week, Eric, the elder of the twins by half an hour, and also the more outgoing, said, 'Grandma, can we call you 'Nanna' like Uncle Orlando's children?'

'Darling, I have *no* objection,' Cobola said. And so, 'Nanna' she became to them all before another week had passed, even to Khadi and Ida.

At fifteen plus, the twins were four years older than their sister, and it was perhaps because they had very little time for her that Adora clung to her grandmother. She curled up on the couch, with her head on Cobola's shoulder, or else sat gazing at her with her father's wide eyes, twisting around her forefinger the long plaits at the ends of the cornrows Khadi did for her on Sunday evenings. After a few minutes, questions would start. One day it was,

'Nanna, Mummy says I got my long hair from you. Where did you get yours from?'

'From my own mother, and *she* got hers from her father. He was a white man, you know. French. My own grandmother was a Susu woman from Guinea. She died when my mother was small and, when he was going back to France, he brought her here to go to school at the convent.'

'Why didn't he take her to France?'

'Because he and my grandmother were not married. In those days, white people didn't marry black people.'

'*Ehn*! Why?

'White people thought it wasn't proper.'

'*Enh*! But they could have children together?'

'Adora, *enough*! It's complicated. I'll explain it when you get older…ya?'

'Okay.'

'And don't say okay when you answer older people…You should always say, yes, so and so, like yes, Nanna.'

'Okay.'

Sighing, Cobola decided to let that go for the time being.

On another day, the question was,

'Nanna, do you mind being old?'

'Sometimes; but I like some things about being old.'

'Like what?'

Adora smiled widely when Cobola made having grandchildren first among the pleasures of growing old. 'And I like not having to work anymore, and not caring what anybody thinks of me…What I *don't* like are the lines on my face, and feeling hairs on my chin, you know, like witches in fairy tales. And I don't like my wrinkled fingers... But most of all, I don't like the aches and pains.'

'Is that why Ida rubs your feet with *ori* every evening?'

'Yes, this ankle and heel hurt me very much sometimes,' Cobola said, sticking out her right foot. 'The *ori* helps.'

As if comforting a friend of her own age or younger, Adora bent down and stroked Cobola's painful foot, saying, with a loving smile, 'Hush, ya.'

Who could resist such charm? By the following Sunday evening when Yao and Isabella telephoned from Accra, Cobola could no longer imagine Adora not being part of her daily life.

Isabella spoke to the children in turn on Eric's mobile phone, while Yao chatted with his mother on hers.

'I'm coming back tomorrow,' he said, 'but only to apply for leave without pay...As we feared, it was cancer, M.A.; but the good news is that it was confined to just one part of the breast. The oncologist says that, according to the lab results, this type of cancer isn't likely to come back, though one can never say never about these things. By the way, the oncologist is a woman...'

'*Enh*! Good for her!'

'Yes. And she's young and beautiful – about Bella's age. She only removed the lump and some of the flesh around it. The reason I'm going to ask for more leave is that she's recommended radiation treatment as well – Monday to Friday for five weeks.'

'Poor Bella!' Cobola said, 'but thank God they didn't have to take off the whole breast.'

'M.A., that was the least of my worries,' Yao said. 'Bella with one breast is better than no Bella.'

'I know, my dear.' Cobola answered, but remembering how much pleasure her husband had taken in her own breasts, she felt like giving Yao another comforting hug.

By the time he arrived on the following Monday, she had turned the situation over in her mind and reached a conclusion.

'Yao, why don't we change places?' she said. 'Let me go to Bella. You know, woman to woman; and I have nursing experience. That way, you won't have to take leave without pay.'

'M.A., stop worrying about the cost,' Yao said. 'Bella has one month's sick leave on full pay, and another month on half pay; and her office will settle most of her medical bills. In any case, *you* are not the one who vowed for better for worse, in sickness and in health. I've decided that she and I are going through this experience together. Besides,' he laughed, 'I'm sure Adora prefers having you here to having me.'

'Nonsense; Adora adores you, and you know it,' Cobola said. 'But it's true that I can stand in for Bella to some extent.'

As she lay in bed later, with Adora snuggled up to her, Cobola thought about Yao's response to her offer and felt proud of him. Trudy was right, she said to herself, I shouldn't have judged him before. Who knows what goes on in private between them, or between any married couple, for that matter? She dropped off to sleep, determined to take Gertrude's advice and mind her own business.

It was just as well that Yao had rejected Cobola's offer to replace him in Accra because two weeks later, after playing with her breakfast, Adora said she didn't feel well enough to go to school.

'What's wrong?' Cobola asked when the boys had gone their way.

'I saw blood on my panties, Nanna; and my stomach hurts.'

'Oh. Has Mummy told you anything about that?'

'Only that it would happen soon and I was to tell her when it did, and I wasn't to be afraid.'

'So you are not afraid.'

'No, Nanna.'

'That's good. It's nothing to be afraid of.'

'But I didn't know what to do. I just put some toilet roll there.'

'Clever girl. Ida will go and buy pads for you this morning; but you have to eat something so I can give you Panadol for your stomach ache, okay?'

As they sat together later, Cobola said,

'Do you know what the blood means?'

'Yes, Nanna – that I can have babies now.'

'And you know how babies are made?'

'Mhm. They taught us that in school.'

'So, from now on you have to be careful around boys, you hear? Don't let any boy touch you down there.'

'Yes, Nanna,' Adora said.

However, Cobola noticed a slight frown creasing her forehead, as if she wasn't sure about the connection between boys touching her 'down there' and the making of babies but felt too shy to ask. Her puzzlement made Cobola wonder how much they really taught them in school, but she decided that giving her more complete information was her mother's responsibility and said no more.

'Oohh, my baby!' Isabella lamented when Cobola called to give them the news, but she cheered up when she heard that Adora had taken the momentous event in her stride, and that she and her grandmother had had a talk about it.

'M.A., thank God you're there!' Isabella breathed. She sounded so unlike her usual overconfident self that Cobola realised just how much the experience of a life-threatening illness had affected her – both of them, in fact. Yao was now doing what she expected a husband to do – taking charge, and Isabella was sounding remarkably humble. With her new determination to mind her own business, Cobola began to think that she might be able to live with them after all, and by the time the five weeks were up and they returned to Freetown, had made up her mind to do so.

On the evening of their arrival, she led the family in a prayer of thanksgiving, then in the humorous tone she always adopted when wanting to make light of a situation, said with genteel formality,

'Mr. and Mrs. Ennison, before we eat, I have an announcement to make. I have decided to accept your kind invitation to share your beautiful home.'

'M.A., that's *wonderful*!' Isabella exclaimed as all the children shouted, 'Yay-ay!' They collapsed with laughter when Yao, having agreed with Isabella, swept Cobola off her feet, grinning from ear to ear. She caused even greater amusement by squealing, 'Put me down! Put me *down!*'

Calm was finally restored and they went to the table. In the course of the meal, Adora said,

'Nanna, can I still sleep with you?'

Yao and Isabella exchanged glances. Aware of a little tension in the air, Cobola answered,

'Darling, I think Mummy and Daddy would like you to be with them now-o… But you can come and sleep with me once in a while…Right?'

She directed the question at Yao and Isabella. Yao's immediate and hearty, '*Of course,*' brightened Adora's crestfallen face. Isabella, too, agreed but only after a slight pause. Cobola noticed the hesitation and warned herself to be careful.

# THREE

Only Abu was in sight when Cobola entered Gertrude's house the next day. He was in his armchair on the veranda, reading a newspaper, with his radio by his side. It was tuned, as usual, to the BBC World Service. They exchanged warm greetings, and he called out, 'Mrs. Kargbo, your person is here-o.'

'And she's ready to eat a small goat,' Cobola added in an equally loud voice.

While not routine, this was not an unexpected visit. She had called Gertrude earlier to say she would come to see her, but would go first to the cemetery to tell Kweku something.

'I'm coming, I'm coming,' Gertrude answered from within the house and bustled in a few minutes later, beaming, sweating, and smelling of hot oil.

'Just in time,' she said. 'I've been frying plantains and fish; Sia has gone to market. Cobs, what will you drink…tea?'

She organised their breakfast before going to change her clothes: fried plantains, small fried snappers and gravy for herself and Cobola, a piece of boiled yam with a steamed snapper for Abu. Abu stared morosely at the teaspoonful of gravy beside his fish.

'You see how your sister is treating me, eh?'

'Abu, it's for your own good,' Cobola said, and firmly refused him the one slice of fried plantain he begged her for. 'I'm not going to encourage you to break your diet. It's for your own good."

Overhearing this exchange as she came to join them, Gertrude said,

'*Thank* you, my sister. He's turned me into a policewoman, then gets annoyed when I do my job.'

'What's wrong with wanting to enjoy my food?' The sharpness of that rejoinder made Cobola jerk on her seat. 'At seventy-nine, how much time do I have left?'

Gertrude's lips tightened, and knowing this was an ongoing argument, Cobola hurriedly said,

'Enough of that. I've come to tell you both that I'm moving to Murray Town.'

'What you should have done two years ago,' Abu answered, and Gertrude concurred.

'The time wasn't right. Now it is.'

'Ah, well, *you* know best,' Abu said.

After his breakfast, he spent a few minutes picking his teeth, before tossing several pills into his mouth and washing them down with water.

'Let me leave you ladies,' he said, and took his mug of coffee to the veranda where his paper and radio waited.

'You see what I have to put up with these days,

eh?' Gertrude complained when she was certain he was out of hearing.

'It must be hard for him, Trudy.'

'I know, but his attitude is bad. I'm only trying to help him to stay well... Anyway, tell me. What made you change your mind about moving?'

'First of all, it was those grandchildren of mine, Adora in particular. Trudy, I can't imagine not seeing and talking to that child every day now. She brushes my hair every afternoon as if I'm a doll – fifty strokes; then she makes two cornrows for me. I appreciate that because I've started feeling pain in my shoulders when lift up my arms. She's taught me how to play Scrabble, and I enjoy it, even though she beats me most of the time. She reads my favourite psalms for me when I ask her to, and she likes to chat. *Questions*!'

'Little girls can be nice-o.' Gertrude said. She and Abu had a daughter, Judith, and two sons, all of whom had emigrated, seeking greener pastures than they thought existed in Sierra Leone – Judith to England with her husband, and Abu junior, and Eddie to the States.

'What else?' she asked.

'Yao and Bella. They've changed since Bella's illness. Yao is behaving like the head of the family now, and Bella seems more…more humble.'

'Are you sure that's not because she's still feeling weak? That by next month she won't be back to the old self that used to annoy you?'

'Somehow, I don't think so, Trudy. I feel it in my heart that both of them have changed.'

'In that case, it's my turn to say, "Praise God Almighty". I never liked you living all that way out of town as if you became an outcast because you were a widow…But be careful-o. Don't get too involved…'

'You think I don't know that?' Cobola answered. 'I will listen, I will help and I will give advice – if and when they ask me. Apart from that, Ida and I will stay in our little corner…That Khadi girl, the one who helps them…She is just too forward for me; and I suspect that she's the kind of person who likes to pass information to and fro. But I know how to handle her.'

'I don't doubt that,' Gertrude said. 'And what about the house at George Town?'

'Yao wants me to sell it. He says going all that way to collect some chicken-change rent will be too much trouble. But *I* am not ready to sell it yet; the rent will be my pocket money…The tenant can take it to him at his office.'

'So, you are set.'

'Mhm. By next week I won't have any more business in George Town… But I miss my favourite taxi driver-o, Trudy – Alimamy. He used to remind me of Kweku when he was young – always cheerful, full of energy and ready to chat. This Sheku Tarawallie, is just the opposite; we never have a proper conversation because he only answers questions. It's either "Yes, madam", "No, madam," or "I don't know, madam". Apart from that, he just drives.'

'Cobs, everybody is different,' Gertrude laughed. 'As long as he drives well.'

'I know, and he does; but he's just too boring for me. It's a good thing that most of the time he doesn't have to drive me far.'

Isabella had another two weeks of sick leave and on the Monday of her final week off work, she knocked on the connecting door to ask Cobola if she minded her company for a while.

'Don't annoy me first thing on a Monday morning-o,' Cobola answered with feigned vexation. 'Come and sit down and tell me how you are…Ida, bring Miss Bella a cup of tea.'

Isabella said, 'I'm feeling much better now, Nanna …'

'Ay-ay, you, too?' Cobola said, laughing.

'That's all we've heard around the house since we came back from Accra,' Isabella said. 'Especially from Adora, so Yao and I have started calling you Nanna, even between ourselves. It's easier…I came to show you the place where I had the operation.'

She had on a pretty floral housecoat and undid enough buttons to expose her left breast. It took all of Cobola's past training as a nurse for her not to gasp. The breast no longer had a nipple; and the skin around Isabella's armpit was a dark reddish colour with an ugly pucker where a jagged scar had formed.

'Hush, ya, my dear!' Cobola said. 'Does it still hurt?'

'Not too much, but I can't wear a bra yet. The surgeon said that will take another two weeks or so.'

'Thank God, you found it in time!'

'Yes, Nanna, I thank God, but…'

To Cobola's dismay, Isabella suddenly buried her face in her hands and, after a moment, began to weep. Cobola did her best to comfort her, but even to her own ears, the words, while sincerely meant, sounded inadequate. In the end, she merely moved closer on the couch, pulled Isabella's head to her shoulder and let her cry. Eventually, Isabella took a handkerchief from her pocket, blew her nose and wiped her streaming eyes.

'I'm sorry,' she said. 'It's Yao.'

'Yao? What has Yao done?'

'Nothing, Nanna. In fact, Yao has been wonderful. The problem is that now, I can't bear it when he tries to touch me.'

That confession brought on more weeping. Isabella pressed both fists into her eyeballs as if to force the tears back, but for several minutes they continued to drench her face and, feeling her distress, Cobola had to wipe her own wet cheeks. Several minutes passed before Isabella exhaled deeply, apologising again.

'Don't worry about me-o,' Cobola said. 'Is Yao complaining?'

'No, Nanna, but he doesn't have to. I know him.'

'You'll get over it, my dear,' Cobola assured her, hoping this was true.

'But how long will he bear with me? That's what is *killing* me.'

Isabella's shaky voice made Cobola say with even greater conviction,

'He will bear with you for as long as it takes. When I was expecting him, his father wasn't allowed to touch me that way because I had had two miscarriages. Yao is like him. Steadfast.'

Again, Cobola was not as confident as she sounded, but what she'd seen of Yao's attitude towards Isabella since their marriage, as well as his recent remarks, had made her think this was probably true.

Still sniffing, Isabella answered, 'He's never been tested in this particular way, Nanna.'

She regained a measure of composure, however, sat up straight, buttoned up her housecoat, drank some tea and, in a welcome change of subject, said,

'Your sons nearly fell out last night.'

Ay-ay! What about?' Cobola said. Yao and Orlando seemed to have formed an easy friendship since they discovered each other, so she couldn't imagine what would have made them come close to quarrelling. Her astonishment increased when Isabella said,

'About you, in a way...I think it was pride on Yao's part, or a bit of jealousy. It hasn't been all that easy for him to share you with Orlando, you know. What happened was that Orlando called to ask how I was, and then offered to rent this part of the house for you. My husband took great objection to that. From what I could gather from Yao's side of the conversation, Orlando couldn't understand why he was refusing his contribution to looking after you...They argued for a few minutes, but Orlando managed to bring him round. He's going to pay Yao a good rent for this place for the next three years. After that, they will review...Nanna, to tell the truth, *I* appreciate the financial help...'

'That's because you are a woman, my dear,' Cobola laughed. 'When it comes to money we need, *we* don't have time for foolish pride...But that was kind of Orlando, eh? After all he's already done for me. Do you think I should call to thank him, or pretend not to know?'

'Pretend not to know, Nanna,' Isabella answered at once and rose to her feet. 'It's better that way; and it's time for me to go. I've disturbed your peace enough for one day.'

'Not at all, my dear; I'm glad you came,' Cobola said. 'I only wish I could do more to help.'

Isabella smiled down at her.

'I feel better getting it off my chest, Nanna... You know my friend, Ilara. She's the person I usually tell my business, but she's never been married. She doesn't understand these things..'

'Well, you came to the right person,' Cobola laughed. 'Between being a midwife for over thirty years, and being married to Yao's father for the same length of time, I know all about these things, so come anytime, you hear?'

On that affectionate note, they hugged and parted.

The moment Isabella left her, Cobola called out to Ida who emerged from her room, dragging her slippers. Cobola disliked such slackness and would normally have reprimanded Ida straightaway; but she was too intent on what she had to say to remark on the misdemeanour.

'I know you heard Miss Bella crying,' she said. 'If you tell Khadi about it, you will be in *big* trouble, you hear me?...And let me tell you,' she went on, wagging a warning finger, 'I will know if you tell her.'

'Nanna, I never tell Sissi Khadi anything.'

'I'm glad to hear that,' Cobola said, but still threw Ida a sceptical glance. 'What happens here, should remain here,'

'Yes, Nanna,'

'Alright, clear these things away, then get ready to go to market. I need more *ori*. And you can ask Khadi if they need anything.'

' Yes, Nanna.'

Ida headed for the kitchen, dragging her slippers in the same irritating way. This time Cobola called her back.

'How many times do I have to tell you to raise your feet when you walk?'

'I'm sorry, ma. I'm not feeling too well.'

32

The thought of pregnancy crossed Cobola's mind, but she promptly dismissed it since, as far as she knew, there was no man in Ida's life. Besides, she had never yet failed to ask for money to buy sanitary pads, which was Cobola's way of monitoring the emptiness, or otherwise, of Ida's womb. She touched Ida's forehead. Her skin was cool to the touch. Nevertheless, Cobola put her on a course of artesunate in case too many malaria parasites in her blood were the cause of her malaise. By the end of the week, Ida seemed to have recovered from whatever had ailed her and Cobola thought no more about it.

After seeing Isabella so completely broken, and sharing confidences with her, Cobola now felt much closer to her daughter-in-law. But she intended to stick to her original plan of maintaining a discreet distance between the two households, which would have been easy, but for Adora. She attended the morning shift at her school, and there used to be only Khadi at home when she returned in the early afternoon. Once she discovered, during her parents' absence, that instead of resting in bed in the afternoons, her grandmother preferred to doze on her couch, she had started bringing her homework next door and staying with Cobola till Khadi called her for her evening meal. Cobola loved this arrangement, but when it happened on the next Thursday and Friday that Isabella sent Khadi to call Adora home, she decided that the cozy afternoons would have to end. She planned to bring up the subject the very next time Adora came to her side of the house, but it was Yao who broached it first. He paid Cobola a surprise visit on the Saturday morning and, after a few minutes of inconsequential conversation, said,

'Nanna, don't take it the wrong way-o, but the main reason I'm here is that Bella isn't too happy about Adora coming to you all the time. She doesn't want to hurt you, so I thought *I* should mention it.'

Cobola sighed. 'My dear, you did the right thing. In fact, I'd already decided to talk to Adora myself...How is Bella doing, by the way? You think she's ready to start work?'

'Oh, yes. As far as recovering from the operation is concerned, she's fine... The only thing is...'

Cobola felt a twinge of dismay, thinking that Yao, too, was about to unburden himself about problems in the bedroom. She preferred not to have to discuss that aspect of his life with her son, yet felt obliged to say, 'The only thing is...?'

To her great relief, Yao answered, 'Nothing for you to worry about, Nanna,' and immediately rose to his feet. 'I have to go. I'm still catching up at the office.'

'I'm sure it hasn't been easy, my dear,' Cobola said as he bent down to kiss her goodbye, 'but you are coping... Right?'

'Yes, Nanna, I'm coping,' he said, though his wry smile suggested otherwise.

'God bless you...ya?'

'Thank you, Nanna. You too.'

Knowing what was probably causing him disquiet, Cobola spent several minutes after his departure in prayer.

# FOUR

The following Monday Adora knocked on her door at the usual time and with her usual question: 'Nanna, can I come?'

Cobola told her she could, but as soon as she entered the room, said, 'Come and sit beside me, darling. We have to talk.'

'Yes, Nanna.'

Adora fixed her wide-eyed gaze upon her.

'How is Mummy?' Cobola asked.

'I think she is fine, Nanna; but she hardly talks these days.'

'That's why *I* want to talk to you. Your visits make me very, very happy, you know that; but now I think Mummy needs you more.'

'She makes me bored, Nanna,' Adora whined, pouting.

'Don't you *ever* say being with your mother makes you bored, you hear me?'

Unaccustomed to harshness from her grandmother, Adora's eyes filled with tears, but Cobola ignored them. 'Mummy has been through a lot. If she's quiet it's because she's not feeling one hundred percent yet. You all have to be more loving to her, not less. Daddy is doing his best, but don't count on Eric and Derek. Boys find such situations awkward. *You* are the one who has to help Mummy, Adora. Even if she doesn't say much, I'm sure she likes having you around.'

'Yes, Nanna,' Adora sniffed, wiping her wet cheeks.

'I'm not saying you shouldn't come here again-o... I still want to you to come, but I don't want Mummy to have to send for you; so, from now on, if she is at home, like over the weekend, you must always ask her if you can come to see me, and for how long.'

'Yes, Nanna.'

'And during the week, like today, you'll have to leave here at four-thirty sharp, so she finds you home when she comes from work. Offer her tea and biscuits and things like that, and then just be with her, unless she says she wants to rest.'

'Yes, Nanna,' Adora said.

Seeing that tears still hovered, Cobola drew her head against her chest for a moment before sending her to do her homework.

'How are things with Adora now?' Gertrude asked.

'Oh, we have adjusted,' Cobola answered. 'She still comes to me every weekday afternoon-o; but I make sure she's back on their side of the house before Bella comes from work.'

Two months had passed. Gertrude was visiting Cobola, who was recovering from a feverish cold, and had brought her friend pepper soup made with cocoyam, beef and salted pigs' feet. Cobola wasn't supposed to eat pigs' feet on account of her high blood pressure, but she could never resist them. Having convinced herself that one or two small pieces wouldn't hurt, she chewed the soft, tasty bones with relish till she remembered how strict she'd been with Abu over one slice of fried plantain. However, the slight pang of guilt she felt then didn't stop her from picking up another one.

'And how is Bella doing?' Gertrude asked.

'She's looking more like her old self again; you know, smartly dressed with her high heels and lipstick, and her hair in those funny twists she makes now that she's stopped relaxing it. But she still seems down.'

'Well, you have to expect that – at least for a while. She's had a bad time. What about Yao?'

'Yao is alright,' Cobola said, but detecting a reservation in her voice, Gertrude gave her an inquiring look.

'It was a heavy blow, Trudy,' Cobola answered vaguely. 'Things had been going so well for them.'

'Do you think it has affected them in bed?'

'Trudy! Aren't you the one always telling me to mind my own business?'

'So? I was only wondering because you didn't sound sure when you said Yao is alright. If *I* had had an operation like that, Abu would have found it hard to behave normally. He is easily put off-o, that man. He might even have found a substitute.'

'God forbid,' Cobola said to herself and steered their conversation in a less disturbing direction.

That same afternoon, Isabella came home from work feeling so exhausted that she fell into a deep sleep after having the tea and biscuits Adora had dutifully brought her. It was twilight when she awoke and, realising Yao would be home any minute, she decided to take a quick shower. She was still in the bathroom when the door opened and Yao said, 'Babes, I'm ho-ome.' In spite of the shower curtain, Isabella instinctively covered her breasts with her hands while calling out a welcome and saying she would soon be with him.

Yao had noticed the gesture through the translucent plastic and, jaded as he felt after the two hours it had taken Sheku to drive the short distance from the city centre to Murray Town, he still decided that this was an opportunity too good to miss. When Isabella's breast had been red and raw from the radiation, she had shown not the slightest hesitation in exposing it to him, but now that it was supposedly healed, she was refusing to let him see her naked – as if he cared what the breast looked like. What he found more troubling was that touching her intimately, even in the dark, had also become taboo. Her behaviour was creating uneasiness between them that, in his opinion, spelled danger for their marriage.

The bathroom door faced his side of the bed. He changed quickly into his house clothes and sat down to wait for Isabella. She appeared a few minutes later, her towel wrapped tightly around her body, from her armpits to her knees. On seeing Yao, she hesitated for a second before stepping out into the room. Yao patted the mattress beside him.

'Babes, come and sit down.'

Again, Isabella hesitated, but she did as he asked.

'I want you to tell me something today,' he said. 'When you were sick, you didn't mind exposing your breast. Why are you hiding it from me now? And why don't you want me to touch you?'

Isabella remained silent.

'Babes, look at me.'

Raising tear-filled eyes, Isabella said,

'Then, you were my nurse and my friend. Now you want to be my husband again...Yao, it's not easy.'

'But Babes, you know I don't care if your breast is twisted or whatever. Your breasts are not you.'

'I know, but I feel so ugly.'

'Does the place still hurt?'

'No. Not anymore.'

'Then let me just hold you...Please. I've missed your body...'

As she had done before, Isabella stiffened when Yao first put his arms around her, but this time, instead of letting her go, he tightened his grip, repeating his plea with such longing that she allowed him to pull her close enough for their foreheads to touch. After a few moments, he murmured,

'Can I kiss you?'

Isabella didn't answer and, taking her silence for consent, Yao tilted her chin and laid his mouth gently on her full, soft lips. They were still cool from the shower, and the lingering fragrance of the soap she used aroused him so powerfully that he was glad to be distracted by a knock on the door. It was Adora, wanting to know if they could start eating or should wait for them.

41

'We are coming right now,' Isabella called through the door, 'but you can start.'

She withdrew from Yao's arms and went to put on one of the kaftans she wore around the house.

'Babes, was that unbearable?' Yao said as he watched her dress.

'No,' Isabella admitted with a rueful smile.

'So I can hope?'

'Yes,' she said, 'but I won't promise.'

Yao, however, detected a hint of the old cockiness in her voice and manner, so that when the generator was turned off and everyone had gone to bed, he said,

'Well?'

'Alright; but with my nightie on.'

'Deal,' he said happily, and reached for her.

Isabella found more pleasure in his deep exhalation as he stopped moving, and in the way he clutched her, murmuring, 'Thanks, Babes', than in the lovemaking itself. But she felt a kind of release, and, for the first time in weeks, slept untroubled by anxious dreams.

They were dressing for work the next morning when she said, 'I was afraid you were going to lose patience with me.'

'And do what?'

'You know; look for consolation elsewhere.'

'I won't lie to you; it crossed my mind once when I was feeling desperate…Do you know what killed the idea? It was something Pops said.'

'Pops? You mean he came to you in a dream?'

'No-o; nothing like that. You know he and I used to talk. When I said I wanted to marry you, he asked why you in particular, and I gave him the reasons. Then he said, " I have only one piece of advice for you. If you want a marriage like mine, be prepared for one hundred percent commitment to your wife – even when it's hard." I liked the way he and Nanna were – always chatting, laughing, teasing each other, holding hands, even when they'd been married for thirty years, so I decided to take his advice…Believe it or not, I've never been unfaithful to you, Bella… But one hundred percent commitment is a two-way street-o. Don't shut me out again; you're not the only one who was afraid.'

Hoping and praying that she would soon accept her disfigurement enough to welcome physical intimacy the way she once did, Isabella gave him her word.

Adora's knock and her 'Nanna, can I come?' startled Cobola out of her afternoon doze.

'Yes, yes, darling, come,' she said, and noticed at once that Adora's expression was brighter than it had been for weeks.

'And how was school today?'

'School was fine, Nanna, and…' Adora's smile stretched almost from one ear to the other. 'I think Mummy is also fine now. She and Daddy were chatting all the way to town. Just like before…'

'Oh, I'm so happy for you all,' Cobola said, clapping her hands with glee. She had a good idea what had restored Isabella's cheerfulness, and to Adora's amusement, raised her arms and eyes towards the ceiling with her usual cry of: 'Prai-aise God almighty!…This calls for a celebration,' she went on. 'Darling, go to the fridge and bring a Maltina for me and a Fanta for you.'

For a while they sipped their drinks in companionable silence, then Adora startled Cobola by saying,

'Nanna, are God and Jesus the same?'

This child will *kill* me, Cobola said to herself, but happily so, for Adora's inquiring mind always delighted her.

'Why do you ask?' she said.

'The teacher who took chapel this morning said so; but then, when she came to the end of her prayer, she said, "Through Jesus Christ our Lord," as if they were separate.'

44

'I, too, used to be confused about that, but I've been reading my Bible more since Uncle Orlando gave me that one with big print...For *me*, God is God. Full stop. Jesus was a special young man and God filled him with His own power. That's why we call him Jesus Christ. The reason God did that was because he wanted to send an important message to the world. The message was that we should love and trust Him with all our hearts and minds and souls. Why? Because *He* loves us like a father and will always take care of us if we obey Him. We are not to worry about *anything*, not even about dying. And we are to treat *everybody* in the world with love and respect because we are all His children – brothers and sisters. Jesus brought the message to the Jews because he was a Jew; and because God's power was in him, he performed miracles as well, and forgave people's sins. The Jewish priests made their Roman rulers kill him in that terrible way because some of what he was telling people went against their own laws and teachings, and he was getting just too popular. Anyway, by the time they killed him he'd done what he'd been sent to do and went straight up to God... '

As always, Adora had given her grandmother her full attention and, when she stopped speaking, said with a thoughtful expression, 'Hmm.' Imagining the wheels of her mind turning, Cobola sensed that she'd soon be asked other questions about Christianity that she'd find more difficult to answer. Indeed, Adora said, 'Nanna, but what about…?'

Cobola held up a restraining hand.

'Don't take my word for anything, you hear? God has given you a good brain. You can work it out for yourself when you grow up…Now go wash the glasses and do your homework so there'll be time to do my hair before you go.'

# FIVE

Cobola had grown fond of Nigerian movies, since moving to Murray. She avoided those that featured sickening occult practices and armed robberies, feeling that they encouraged harmful ideas in the community, but she enjoyed many of the true to life family dramas in which good always overcame evil in the end. She even had her favourite movie stars, among them, Patience Ozokwor, a fine actress, who often played misguided souls – wicked mothers-in-law or flighty middle-aged women with no sense of dignity. She was engrossed in a Patience Ozokwor vehicle one evening in August when Khadi called her on her mobile.

'Nanna, I want to come and see you, ma.'

The tone of voice in which Cobola answered, 'Now?' made it quite clear that a visit would be most unwelcome. Khadi said hurriedly,

'I can wait till tomorrow, ma. It is not so urgent.'

'Yes. Tomorrow will be better. Come around ten o'clock when everybody has gone.'

'Do you know what Khadi wants to see me about?' she asked Ida, who was watching the movie with her.

'No, ma,' Ida answered, but she seemed uncomfortable. Cobola gave her one hard look before returning to the story where, having received her just deserts, the Patience Ozokwor character had lost her mind and was rolling around in the dust, crying out in agony as she scratched intense, but imaginary, itches all over her body. Cobola always became thoroughly involved in the movies she watched, particularly when they were as well acted as this one had been.

'Serves her right! Wicked woman,' she said with grim satisfaction before telling Ida to turn off the television.

The next morning, Khadi turned up as expected, but spent several irritating minutes beating about the bush before saying,

'Nanna, it is Ida who sent me to you, ma.'

'Which Ida?...You mean the one that lives here with me?'

'Yes, ma.'

'Ida!' Cobola shouted. 'Come here right now.'

She raised her voice again when Ida made a reluctant appearance. 'What nonsense is this? You are sending messages to me when we live under the same roof?'

Ida remained silent, her head bowed. Stronger suspicions about pregnancy made Cobola examine her more closely this time, but Ida seemed just the same pretty, though rather shapeless, young woman she'd always been.

'What do you want Khadi to tell me?'

'That she is expecting, ma,' Khadi said, obviously anticipating a drama from which she intended to drain the last drop of enjoyment. Cobola was determined to thwart her.

'Alright, Khadi,' she said calmly, 'I have heard. Thank you.'

Khadi hung back. Cobola thanked her again, this time with such finality in her voice that Khadi had no alternative but to leave the room. Thinking she might be lingering in the corridor to hear what happened next, Cobola told Ida to reopen the door and keep it slightly ajar. Only then did she react to the news.

'And who is the father?'

It took Ida so long to open her mouth that she yelled,

'Talk!'

'Nanna... it is Sheku, ma.'

'*Sheku*? You mean Mr. Yao's driver?'

'Yes, ma.'

First, Cobola's jaw dropped; then, she let out a cackle at the thought of that man of few words successfully seducing Ida. Wonders will never cease, she said to herself, and aloud, 'Did he force you?'

'No, ma.'

Indeed, Cobola would have been more shocked to hear that Sheku had forced himself on Ida. Apart from his taciturnity, she had never observed the slightest gleam in his eye to suggest that he was capable of mischief, let alone the serious wickedness of sexual assault.

'How many times have you missed your period?'

'Four times, ma.'

'*What!* And every month you came to me for money to buy pads? Deceitful girl! I have the good mind to tell you to pack your things and leave my house today.'

Tears were already streaming down Ida's cheeks. On hearing that threat, she fell on her knees, sobbing, and clutched Cobola's feet in the time-honoured gesture of entreaty.

'Please, ma, I beg. It was only because I was too ashamed to tell you. I beg.'

Though the circumstances were entirely different, Cobola had found herself in a similar situation sixty years earlier. Remembering how she had felt at the time, she said more kindly,

'Alright, get up, get up. Tomorrow, you'll start going to the clinic. For now, go and finish your work.'

'God bless you, ma,' Ida gushed. 'God bless you.'

As soon as she left the room, Cobola telephoned Gertrude.

'How could I have missed a four-month pregnancy, Trudy?' she lamented. 'Me. A midwife for over thirty years?'

'Old age, ' Gertrude answered in her matter-of-fact way. 'And Ida has been with you for a very long time; maybe she has become like part of the furniture.'

'Trudy, don't say that; I feel bad enough already. I'll have to talk to Yao and Bella this evening and decide what to do. '

Trying to be helpful, Gertrude said,

'Perhaps Sheku will marry her.'

'Suppose he has a wife already? You know he doesn't talk; I haven't bothered to ask him.'

'Whatever the case may be, let's hope he'll be willing and able to support the child.'

'Let's hope so.'

Following a message sent to them by Adora, Yao and Isabella came to see Cobola that evening and, since she'd never summoned them before, greeted her with some apprehension.

'My dears,' she said when they were sitting down, 'We have a situation-o. Ida is pregnant – four months.' She couldn't resist pausing for dramatic effect before going on. 'She says Sheku Tarawallie is the father.'

Yao and Isabella exchanged astonished glances, exclaiming almost in unison, 'Ay-Ay!' Isabella went on, 'In the short time he's been here?' and Yao, 'Sheku who acts as if butter won't melt in his mouth?'

'Be that as it may,' Cobola said, 'Ida is pregnant.'

Relieved that the situation had nothing to do with his mother's health, always a concern with him, Yao visibly relaxed.

'Well,' he said, 'I'll tell him tomorrow, Nanna – that is if he doesn't know already; and I'll ask him his intentions. But I'm curious,' he went on after a pause, 'Where do you think they did it?'

'Yao!' Isabella said with a reproving frown, 'In front of Nanna?'

Yao hurriedly apologised, but far from being offended, this little exchange amused and reassured Cobola, suggesting as it did that things were truly back to normal between the two of them. Bella is a brave girl, she thought, before answering Yao, straight-faced,

'It must have been in your Volvo, my dear. It's big enough at the back, and it was always here when you people were in Accra. So was Sheku. For Adora's safety, if I wasn't going out, I used to send Ida with him when he took her to school and brought her back. That must have been how the romance began.'

Yao had acquired his classy, blue-grey Volvo from a departing diplomat and, more than five years later, it remained his pride and joy. The two women looked at each other and spluttered with laughter when he said with a look of distaste, 'I hope not.'

The next morning, he called Cobola from his office.

'Nanna, good news. Sheku hasn't denied it. He says he wants to marry Ida because he knows her madam has taught her how to behave, how to cook, and how to keep a house clean.'

'Sheku said all that? *Sheku Tarawallie?*'

'Yes,' Yao answered, laughing. 'It shows he can talk when he wants to. I'll bring him to your place this evening to discuss the matter further.'

Cobola sighed with relief when Yao rang off. There were thousands of young men in the city finding it hard enough to maintain themselves, let alone children, so it hadn't surprised her to hear that many of them simply had their fun and moved on to the next conquest, taking no responsibility for consequences. Sheku, therefore, went up in her estimation, though she still eyed him with strong disapproval when he entered her sitting-room that evening.

'Bad boy!' she said. 'So that's what you've been up to – leading Ida astray.'

Avoiding her reproachful eyes, Sheku mumbled,

'I'm sorry, madam. I have told Mr. Yao that I want to marry her.'

'I'm glad to hear that. No doubt, her people will agree, so we'll arrange a day and time for you to bring your own people for her with kola. But after that, I want you to take her to the registry, or a mosque or church, you hear me? I want to see a paper that says you have married her.'

'Yes, madam.'

'And let me warn you,' Cobola went on in the same stern tone. 'Don't let me see her with a swollen face because you knocked her-o. Otherwise, you'll have to answer to me.'

'Yes, madam,' Sheku said, still keeping his gaze on her rug.

It was later decided that Ida would continue working for Cobola for as long as she could, coming in every day except Sunday, and that during the week, Sheku would have his main meal at the Murray Town house. Cobola had no objection to Ida coming to work with her baby when it arrived. In fact, having always loved babies, she looked forward to having one in the house every day.

It was Isabella herself who suggested that Adora sleep in Ida's room when it became vacant, saying, 'So Nanna won't be all alone at night.' Adora jumped for joy and, in the privacy of her bedroom, Cobola hummed an old calypso tune and, laughing at herself, moved her body the way she'd seen elderly women do it in Nigerian movies when they received welcome news.

# SIX

Campaigning for general elections had been going on for several months with the usual hullaballoo of mass rallies where supporters and non-supporters alike showed up either in red or green T-shirts, depending on the party concerned. Music blasted from speeding vehicles, songs composed for the campaign were either insulting or flattering, again depending on whose supporters were singing them; and, of course, promises and more promises, which a cynical electorate no longer believed would amount to anything once the elections were over. In the relative backwater that was Murray Town, most of this passed Cobola by, but she went to cast her vote in their constituency. The first presidential poll was inconclusive. She cast her vote again at the run-off, and was pleased when her candidate for president was declared the clear winner. Isabella, who refused to have anything to do with politics, never took part in General Elections, but Yao had voted for the same candidate and party as his mother, grumbling that he'd only done so for want of a better choice. He certainly didn't share her pleasure in the new president's handsome face and imposing figure.

'Nanna, what do his face and figure have to do with governing the country well?' he asked, giving her a look of exasperation.

'Nothing, my dear,' Cobola laughed, 'I'm just glad we now have a young president who is very nice to look at and who, unlike the previous one, seems strong and healthy as well. He gives me hope.'

Yao made a sceptical snort, but Cobola's optimism remained high – with good reason, as it turned out, at least in the months following the elections. Weeks went by without the need to run the generator every day, such had been the improvement in the power supply; and there was soon evidence of efforts to revive long-derelict mines in the provinces and improve the country's deplorable roads. Within a year of the General Elections, however, frequent blackouts were once again the norm in parts of the city, though less so in others, including theirs, and rumours of rampant corruption resurfaced; but since more energetic efforts seemed to be being made to tackle this scourge, Cobola refused to admit that Yao's pessimism had been well founded.

Meanwhile, after running their charitable clinic for four consecutive years, Orlando and Beverly West had decided, with considerable regret, that their present sojourn in Sierra Leone would be their last. They told the family in Freetown, that fundraising, organising their trips, the long journeys to and from Sierra Leone, as well as the ever-increasing number of patients, had begun to take their toll on Beverly's health.

'And Nanna,' Orlando said, 'as I told you once before, I'm not a missionary. Living and working here is *hard*. We admire you Sierra Leoneans.'

He had hoped to lessen his mother's disappointment by saying that, all being well, he and Beverly would come to celebrate her eightieth birthday with her, but Cobola answered with a childish pout,

'That's no consolation. Who knows whether these old bones will last another four years?'

'Nanna, they'll last much longer than that,' Orlando assured her. In a further attempt to make her smile, he added that he'd seen the future in her stars. Cobola dismissed that remark with a snort. But she wouldn't be saying goodbye to the Wests for several weeks yet. Their second son, Michael, was getting married after Christmas and he wanted her there. Having his parents' assurance that winters in Atlanta were usually mild, she had agreed to go to the States with them and stay until mid-January.

By this time, Ida had gone to live with Sheku and Adora had taken over the evening chore of massaging Cobola's feet. Two weeks before their departure for the States, Adora's slim fingers were busy with this task when she said,

'Nanna, I have a *big* surprise for you.'

'*Enh!*'

'Yes. You'll know what it is at the dinner Mummy and Daddy are having for your birthday and to say goodbye to Uncle Orlando and Auntie Beverly.'

'Not even a hint?'

'Not even a hint; and you won't guess, so don't even try.'

'Alright-o,' Cobola chuckled. 'At least I know it will be a nice surprise.'

For the dinner, Khadi and Isabella served the superb dishes that always reminded Cobola of the food they had sent the day Orlando came to hear why she had given him up for adoption. The Jollof Rice and its accompaniments were just as delicious, and this time, Isabella had added to the menu a well seasoned baked barracuda tail, and a pork pot roast with potatoes, mixed vegetables and plenty of gravy. It was a buffet meal, and having served himself, Orlando had begun to eat before sitting down and, sighing rapturously. He said with a rapturous sigh,

'This is one thing I'm going to miss about coming here, Bella. Good home cooking, especially yours.'

Not at all put out that her husband was complimenting another woman's expertise in the kitchen, Beverly said, to Isabella,

'It's true, honey. In our house, we eat ready-made meals most of the time; just heat them in the microwave, and they're ready to go.'

'But they taste very good,' Cobola said tactfully.

'Yes, but not like this, Nanna.' Beverly answered. 'This gravy is pure heaven. It reminds me of my Aunt Alicia's cooking…Honey, you remember Aunt Alicia's pot roast?'

'*Unforgettable*,' Orlando answered between mouthfuls. 'And her meat loaf was just as yummy.'

Conversation moved from one topic to another, including the twins' higher education. Orlando and Beverly raised their eyebrows when Eric said they wanted to study medicine.

'Wow! That will cost you,' Orlando said to their parents.

'Not so much if they go to COMAHS,' Yao answered.

'Which is?'

'Oh; sorry. COMAHS is our local medical school, in full, College of Medicine and Allied Health Sciences. After their basic training, they could go to Ghana, Kenya, or perhaps South Africa, to specialise. We'll see.'

'The thing is to work as hard as you can, starting now,' Orlando advised the boys. 'With excellent grades, your options improve. Who knows? You might even get some kind of post-graduate scholarship.'

'That's what we keep telling them.' Isabella said and, with a tender glance in their direction, went on, 'they're both doing very well, I must say.'

'That's great!' Orlando said. 'Keep it up, guys. I'll do some research when I get back; see if there's anything on offer for undergraduate studies.' But seeing the way the twins' faces lit up, he warned, 'Don't get your hopes up, though. It's not easy these days.'

'You hear that?' Yao told them, 'COMAHS it is.'

The twins slouched low in their seats, their expressions making it clear that the prospect of COMAHS didn't excite them in the least.

'You boys don't know how lucky you are,' Cobola chimed in. 'Your grandpa would have been so happy if there'd been COMAHS in his day. He, too, wanted to become a doctor, you know, and he had the brains for it. He gave up the idea only because there was no money to send him overseas and he wasn't lucky enough to get a scholarship.'

She realised this discussion on the twins' future had been going on for some time when Isabella said pointedly, 'You hear that? Be grateful for COMAHS. Okay?'

Her words had little effect on the boys' demeanour, however – not until Khadi brought in the dessert and they saw that, as well as a Madeira cake for their grandmother, there was also a vanilla cheese cake, which was their own favourite. They sat up straight then and grinned at each other, knowing that their mother would give them extra large helpings.

Having risen to sing the birthday song for Cobola, the family resumed their seats, all except Yao who struck a glass with a knife and announced that Miss Adora Ennison was about to perform a song she had practised as a special send-off present for Uncle Orlando and Auntie Beverly, and as a birthday present for Nanna. *A song,* Cobola said to herself in happy anticipation. She had heard Adora singing snatches of popular tunes around the house, but it was heart-warming to think she had taken the time and trouble to memorise and practise an entire song for their pleasure.

Adora stood up and moved shyly to the centre of the room. She was looking particularly pretty that evening, showing off gentle-curves in slim-fitting jeans and a short-sleeved pink blouse. She had been to the hairdresser with her mother in the morning and, as a result, instead of her usual cornrows, glossy ringlets caressed her cheeks. She glanced in her parents' direction. Her mother smiled, and her father gave her an encouraging wink. She clasped her hands before her and took a deep breath.

Cobola couldn't have been more astonished or delighted when out of Adora's slim throat soared a female version of Kweku Ennison's voice.

> *O Lord my God, when I in awesome wonder,*
> *consider all the worlds thy hand has made,*
> *I see the stars, I hear the rolling thunder,*
> *Thy power throughout universe, displayed.*

Even before Adora came to the end of the first two lines, Cobola had begun to feel as if her heart would leap from her chest, so powerful were the emotions surging within her: pleasure in the purity of Adora's voice, a deep feeling of tenderness towards her granddaughter, but above all, joy such as she hadn't experienced since the day Orlando re-entered her life.

Adora raised her arms, threw her head back and started on the chorus,

*Then sings my soul, my saviour Lord to Thee,*
*How great thou art, how great thou art:*
*Then sings my soul, my saviour Lord to thee;*
*How great thou art, how great thou art!*

Eric nudged Derek.

'Look, Nanna is crying.'

Indeed, tears were streaming down their grandmother's cheeks as Adora sang out the final phrase with the full power of her lungs.

'Darling, that was *wonderful!*' Cobola said, clapping vigorously, 'Thank you. Thank you!'

As the rest of them joined in the applause, Orlando said,

'Another Whitney Houston coming up.'

Beverly readily agreed; so did Eric and Derek in a teasing, big-brotherly fashion, while Yao and Isabella exchanged pleased glances; but Cobola, who had rapidly regained her composure, said in a firm voice.

'Not Whitney Houston, Orlando, though I love hearing her sing. Adora's voice is like her grandfather's. Most of you never heard him sing, but he had the most *beautiful* voice. Even though all of you sing much, much better than me, neither you, Yao, nor both of you, Eric and Derek, inherited that voice. I've always felt sorry about that; but I heard it again when Adora was singing just now. That's why I cried; I was crying for joy. Darling, come here, let me hug you. What a shame that they still don't allow women to sing in the Cathedral choir!'

Adora melted into her arms, and Cobola asked, 'But *how* did you manage to keep it a secret?'

'Mummy and Daddy let me practise in their bathroom,' Adora told her with a giggle.

'It was the farthest place from your side of the house, Nanna,' Isabella added. 'We were sure no sound would reach you from there.'

'And you were right. I never heard a thing… Wonderful!'

Exhausted all of a sudden by the intensity of her emotions, Cobola gave Adora another squeeze and gestured her away, saying, 'Let me go to bed, ya; otherwise, I won't be fit to travel tomorrow…'

Once on her feet, she said, 'Well, good night, my dears...Bella, as usual your food was first class.' Influenced by her visits to America, she added with a wave, 'Love you all,' before moving towards the door.

Yao said, 'Let me see you home, Nanna… Adora will come soon…'

As they crossed the short corridor to her side of the house, he asked fondly, 'You okay?'

'Very okay, my dear; this has been my best birthday for a long time. I just need to rest.'

'Yes-o, the next two days are going to be hectic – Freetown to Amsterdam, Amsterdam to Atlanta.'

'Not to mention going through registration and immigration here and immigration over there; but once we get to Orlando's house, I intend to take things very easy until the wedding.'

# SEVEN

On a Wednesday evening in the middle of January, Cobola went into Yao's arms at Lungi International Airport feeling slightly let down that only he had come to meet her. She hadn't expected to see Isabella but had hoped Adora or the twins would be with him.

'Nanna, it was easier to come straight from the office,' Yao explained when she made light mention of it. They were now in one of the taxis that ran between the airport and the ferry terminal at Tagrin Point. 'Sheku is waiting for us at Government Wharf.'

'So we are going by the government ferry?'

'Mhm.'

'Oh, I'm so glad!' Cobola said, instantly forgetting her little disappointment. This time they would be using a large, stable vessel instead of one of the privately owned speedboats that were the only other means of crossing the mouth of the Sierra Leone River to Freetown. With her stiff ankle, she hated getting on and off their wobbly decks.

'And how are our young parents-to-be?' she asked after a while.

'Fine, I think,' Yao answered. 'You know Sheku doesn't say much.'

'And all is well at Murray Town?'

'All is well, Nanna. Bella is due for her one-year check-up, so she'll be going to Accra next week; but we are not worried about it. The boys are studying hard, and Adora has started taking singing lessons at Ballanta Academy. You'll be surprised at how mature that child has become in the short time you've been away. She offered to clean your place because Ida can't do hard work anymore. According to Bella, she did a good job.'

'That's my girl,' Cobola said fondly.

Half an hour later, they were settled in the ferry and trundling across the water towards Government Wharf. The sun had almost set but, despite the dimming light, Cobola was still able to enjoy Freetown's landmarks as they went past: Kissy Ferry Terminal, Queen Elizabeth II Quay, where some large container ships were berthed, Mount Aureol with the tall Kennedy Building silhouetted against the sky, part of Tower Hill, and all the little bays. Finally, sighing with contentment that she was home, she turned to Yao who had not spoken since calling Isabella to announce her safe arrival.

'So what's the bad news you are keeping from me? And don't tell me there's no bad news because for the last two weeks I've had an uneasy feeling. And you look pulled down; you've even lost weight.'

That last remark made Yao laugh.

'Nanna, that's your imagination playing tricks,' he said. 'Maybe I look pulled down, but I haven't lost any weight. There's been a bit of trouble at work, but it only started yesterday.'

'Enh. What is it?'

'Long story.'

'Give me a hint, at least.'

'No,' Yao said firmly. 'Rest first. And don't worry, it's not that serious. I'm not about to be sacked or anything like that.'

'Thank God!'

He put an arm around his mother's shoulders, showing his dimple.

'I'm glad you are back-o,' he said. 'I always feel good when I know you're around and praying for me.'

'Nanna!' Adora screamed as they entered the house sometime later. She was the first to reach Cobola and almost knocked her over, so fierce was her embrace. Isabella followed, her welcome just as warm, though much more sedate. Then the boys took turns to give Cobola one-armed hugs like grown men.

'Aah!' she breathed, as she sank unto her couch after the greetings. 'It's so good to be back.'

'Nanna, I like your trousers-o,' Derek said. 'Trendy.'

'Darling, the trousers were for warmth, not for fashion,' Cobola laughed. 'You know I travelled via Amsterdam. I knew it would be cold in the airport. Not like Atlanta.'

'Khadi made pepper soup for you,' Isabella said.

'Thank you, my dear, I'll eat it tomorrow; right now a cup of Milo will do me just fine.'

'What about your feet, Nanna?' Adora asked, eager to please. 'Don't they need a rub with *ori*?'

Her feet could, indeed, have done with a shea butter massage, but Cobola said,

'Thank you, darling, but let's leave that, too, till tomorrow. All I need now is my bed – after the Milo.'

So, they said goodnight and left her – all except Adora who, now that her grandmother was home, had already brought her pyjamas over to sleep in what was still referred to as 'Ida's room'. She made Cobola's Milo and helped her change the SIM card on her mobile phone before kissing her goodnight.

While she waited for her Milo to cool, Cobola called Gertrude to announce her arrival.

'Cobs, Abu is not well-o.' Gertrude said at once. 'His heart.'

'No wonder I had that bad feeling!' Cobola exclaimed. 'I thought it was something to do with

Yao and his family. Why didn't you tell me when we spoke last week?'

'And spoil the rest of your stay when there was nothing you could do? Anyway, he's not too bad, but the doctor says he has to stay in bed for at least one more month.'

'*What*! I'll come tomorrow,' Cobola said.

'Anh-anh, I beg you. Rest first,' Gertrude answered. 'I don't want two patients on my hands.'

'Alright, Friday – after I've been to the cemetery. Meanwhile, tell Abu I say he should behave himself.'

That troubling news, coupled with maternal concern for Yao, prevented Cobola from relaxing enough to fall asleep immediately after her prayers and her affirmation that goodness and mercy would follow her all the days of her life. Consequently, after drinking the cup of tea Adora brought before setting off for school, she decided to spend the day in bed. Ida telephoned her later, full of apologies that she hadn't felt well enough to come to work that day. Cobola told her not even to think of returning until her baby was six weeks' old.

'After all,' she said, 'I still have two good hands, and I can move around. Besides, Khadi and Adora are here; they will help me in their spare time.'

Indeed, having been put firmly in her place over the announcement of Ida's pregnancy, Khadi was now careful not to pass on gossip, or to be too forward. Within those boundaries, the two women had had some pleasant conversations. Cobola had discovered that not only was Khadi a widow like herself, her late husband having been a soldier killed in action during the Rebel War, but also that she had only one child – a son born after several miscarriages. As a result of those coincidences, and the change in her behaviour, Cobola now felt so kindly disposed towards Khadi that she had brought her presents from America: costume jewellery, a handbag, and a shirt for her son.

Feeling sufficiently rested after her day in bed, Cobola rose early enough to do the morning rounds with the family – taking Adora to school, Isabella to her office, and Yao to his. Sheku would then drive her to Ascension Town Cemetery to tell Kweku she was back, and on to Wilkinson Road to see Gertrude and Abu.

On their way to Isabella's office, Yao said,

'Nanna, I'll come and tell you all about that business tomorrow morning.'

'What business?' Isabella asked.

'The problem at work.'

'Much ado about nothing,' Isabella said, sucking her teeth.

Her dismissive remark lessened Cobola's anxiety but not her curiosity. Knowing that all would be revealed the next day, however, she put the matter out of her mind.

Of late she'd been finding the uneven paths between the graves more difficult to navigate, so she asked Sheku to help her. Not to be thought too familiar, he held her delicately by her wrist as he followed her directions to Kweku's grave and, once past the silk cotton trees, promptly released her hand and moved off to wait at a discreet distance. After her usual preliminaries, Cobola said,

'Kweku, I am back from America-o, and I am happy to be home. They said the weather wouldn't be cold, but it was too cold for me sometimes. My foot made me suffer, even though I took my tablets and wore socks day and night, except when I went to the wedding. Anyway, I enjoyed myself…Yao has had a problem at work, but I think it's over now; he says he will tell me about it tomorrow. And all is well with Bella and your grandchildren. Adora, sings as well as you, and she's now taking lessons. We thank God…'

73

Just as she was saying, 'Rest in peace, ya?' Pa Cowan came running up to greet her.

'Happy new year, ma. Let God keep you well.'

Cobola returned the greeting, and handed him not only his annuity but also a new year's tip which he vehemently denied would be spent on local gin.

'I am a changed person, ma,' he stammered. 'Ask anybody. My wife took me to one crusade before Christmas. The pastor put his hand on my head and prayed for me to stop drinking. Now I only take one tot a day – just to warm my bones. This work is not easy-o.'

Cobola could have pointed out that he still reeked of alcohol, but she didn't, merely saying, before calling out to Sheku to help her back to the car, 'I know it's not easy to change bad habits. I will pray for you, ya?'

She went up the Kargbos' steps announcing her arrival.

'I'm here-o. The wanderer is back.'

It was Sia, their helper, who answered the door.

'Where is Gramma?'

'Inside, ma. She is feeding Grampa. I will tell her you have come.'

'Feeding Grampa'. That phrase rang such an alarm bell that tears stung Cobola's eyes. Gertrude, however, seemed quite cheerful when she appeared about ten minutes later.

'I'm doing bedside nursing again, after all these years', she said.

'How is he?' Cobola asked as they hugged each other.

'Go and see for yourself.'

Abu was propped up on three pillows. He seemed to be breathing normally but his cheeks had lost their healthy sheen.

'And so I face the final curtain,' he said by way of a greeting.'

It was a line from a song both couples had loved in the 1970s, and to which they once sang along lustily when a few beers had gone down.

'What final curtain?' Cobola scoffed, though, from the look of Abu, she thought that might well be true. 'You are going to get up from that bed.'

'If you say so; but *I* know how I'm feeling... Anyway, welcome; and happy new year.'

Cobola returned to the sitting-room feeling so despondent that she sat down at the table with a heavy sigh, resting her cheek on her hand. Her spirits were only restored when Sia brought in a dish with freshly-made *moy-moy*. The ground black-eyed beans had been prepared just the way she liked them, steamed with groundnut oil, hot peppers, lots of chopped onion, some smoked fish and a dash of tomato puree to give it an appetising colour.

'Trudy, this is one of the reasons I love you,' she said, and mouthed a kiss at her friend as she helped herself. 'You always know what to do or say to make me smile.'

'Abu depressed you, eh? But the doctor is sure he will recover this time. It's his mind that's making him look so sick. And there is nothing I can do about that except pray for him.'

'I'll help you pray', Cobola said and went on, 'You know, sometimes I'm glad Kweku didn't become an old man. Who knows what that accident saved him from?'

'Yes-o,' Gertrude said. 'God knows best… Anyway, enough of this heavy talk. Gist me about your grandson's wedding.'

'Let me come and sit beside you,' Cobola said. 'I have pictures. They had to print them especially for me because they all put their photos in their computers and look at them like slides or videos.'

'They can do that here now-o,' Gertrude said. 'Even this your backward country is moving with the times. Judith wanted to send me a computer so we can contact each other by email. She says it's much cheaper than using the mobile.'

'That is true, but you'll have to learn how to type – at least with two fingers; and there are many little things to remember. It's worth it, if you persevere.'

Unimpressed, Gertrude said, 'I've told her I don't want it. I like to hear her voice, and I can't be bothered to start learning new things now... In any case, half the time the electricity is off. Show me pictures, ya.'

The first photograph was of the rehearsal dinner which took place after everyone involved in the wedding had been to the church to practise their part. Cobola pointed out the bride, Suzanne, and her parents, and set that photograph aside.

'Look at this one of the church,' she said, 'There are people whose business is organising events. Suzanne's parents hired a wedding planner. She and her people decorated the church...Look...'

Huge urns containing fresh white flowers had been placed in the empty spaces around the altar. The aisle end of every pew had a large,white, organza rosette tied to it, and at every other pew, a stand, about three feet tall, held a glowing white candle.

'Hey-ey!' Gertrude exclaimed. 'Wonderland!'

'I'm telling you!' Cobola said as she shuffled the pictures. 'This is Ronald, Orlando's older son, walking me to my seat. Grandparents came in before parents; Suzanne still has her grandma and grandpa. After taking me to my seat, Ronald had to go outside again because he was one of the groomsmen.'

'Cobs, you really did it for them in that lavender *bubu*. Orlando must have been proud of his African mother.'

'It's nice, eh? Bella had it made for me. Everyone admired the embroidery.'

'But were you not cold?'

'Only when we went outside to take pictures, and even then, it was only my arms. The church and the reception hall were warm enough, and I had on tights – there they call them panty-hose. Beverly had also given me a woolen vest with sleeves, and some funny woolen drawers that reached almost to my ankles. I was okay… Look at Beverly and Orlando…'

Orlando was dressed in a well-fitting black tuxedo with a beautiful buttonhole. His maroon bowtie and cummerbund blended well with Beverly's rose-coloured dress and glamorous hat.

'So they know how to swank,' Gertrude said, surprised and admiring. 'Here, they were always so simple.'

'Trudy, they came to work, not to show off,' Cobola said. 'After the parents and grandparents were on their seats, the groomsmen entered the church and stood in a row on one side of the altar.

They were dressed like Orlando except that their own cummerbunds and bowties were green.'

'Five of them?' Gertrude exclaimed as she gazed at the next photograph.

'Mhm,' Cobola said, showing her another picture. 'And five bridesmaids.' The young women were dressed in pale yellow satin dresses, floor-length, with tight-fitting sleeves. Their white bouquets had plenty of small leaves of the same shade of green as the groomsmen's cummerbunds and bowties. 'All this time the organ had been playing lovely music-o. The bridesmaids, too, came in one by one and stood in a row on the other side of the altar. By now the church was *full*. You should have seen the hats! Better than the Cathedral on Easter Sunday in those days. Fortunately, it didn't rain…All you could hear for a while was rustling, whispered conversation, and the organ music; then at the exact time Suzanne was supposed to arrive, the organ suddenly blasted like military bugles, and everybody stood up. The page boy and flower girl came in first…Look at them. Cute, eh?… The flower girl's small basket was full of rose petals. She scattered them on the aisle carpet for Suzanne to walk on; and don't you think Suzanne looked like a princess in a fairy tale? Her bouquet was white with just a few green leaves showing here and there…Look. Tears filled my eyes while she was coming down the aisle on her father's arm, Trudy. Michael's heart must have been beating like one of those small drums.'

'As for you!' Gertrude said. 'Madam Romantic. It's all those books you used to read.'

'And what's wrong with being romantic?'

'Nothing,' Gertrude said, but in a tone that made it plain she couldn't care less about romance.

'The service itself was so short I couldn't believe it,' Cobola went on. 'No hymns and no sermon, just a few encouraging words from the priest. And there were four other interesting things. One: the couple had written their own vows; none of that for better for worse in sickness and in health. They just smiled into each other's eyes and talked about their love and promised to take care of each other. Two: after the vows, they went up to a small table in front of the altar with their mothers. The table had three candles side by side. Each mother lit a candle and handed it to her child. Suzanne and Michael then lit the middle candle together. That was to signify the union of two families. Three: after the priest had pronounced them man and wife and they had kissed, the groomsmen put a nicely decorated broom with a long handle on the ground in front of them. They had to jump over it, holding hands… Here is the picture. They say it's a custom from the days of slavery. And four: there was no signing of the register to bore people. The whole thing took less than one hour.'

'No doubt, that pleased Cobola. You always complain about our long, long weddings.'

'You've said it...'

'But when did they sign the register?' Gertrude asked.

'When the service was over and we had all gone to the church hall for the reception. Apparently, only the best man and maid of honour signed the register with them; then they went outside to take pictures.'

'So, not even the parents signed.'

'Not even the parents. I was surprised...Look at the way the church hall was decorated,' Cobola went on, showing Gertrude another photograph. 'Look at the table cloths and the flowers, and the draped chairs with big bows on the backs, and all those yellow and white balloons and garlands. It was like Fairy Land...Don't believe anyone who tells you that money isn't sweet.'

'Hmm. I wonder what millionaires' weddings are like over there?'

'Yes-o. They must be out of this world... When we were all sitting down – I was on the high table with the other grandparents and the parents –

again the bridesmaids and groomsmen came in first, one by one. Michael had said he wanted to include one African tradition, so I had offered to give them water. Orlando took me to meet them at the door. I said the usual words, and they drank from the glass before entering the hall... Here is the picture. Another thing I liked was that there were only three speeches, and all short: the best man, the chief bridesmaid – there they say maid-of-honour, and the bridegroom. Then we had dinner. That was the only part I didn't enjoy. They had a roasted piglet and plenty of other food, but nothing was tasty enough for me. I missed Bella's Jollof and a rich Sierra Leone salad, and rice bread, and your ginger beer. The cake, too, I didn't like – too soft, too sweet.'

'But it was *beautiful-o*,' Gertrude said as she gazed at a photograph of a round, white, three-tiered cake, with a spray of yellow roses flowing down one side from top to bottom.'

'Did they dance?' she asked.

'*Mhm!* The DJ played nice music. Orlando took me for a slow piece and so did Ronald and Michael. By that time, Suzanne had removed her veil and train so she could move around freely and dance and chat. After a while, Michael knelt down, raised her skirt and removed her garter from her leg – another of their customs. Then, he stood up with his back towards a group of his unmarried friends and threw the garter. The person that catches it is supposed to be the next bridegroom, so some of his friends did their best to avoid it, which was funny. On the other hand, when Suzanne turned her back and threw her bouquet for an unmarried woman to catch, they all tried hard to catch it so they could be the next bride…That part was also funny. Around eight o'clock, Michael and Suzanne left for their honeymoon, and we all went to the entrance to throw raw rice at them for good luck and fertility before they drove away. Trudy, by then I was so fagged out, I could hardly stand. Apart from everything else, all the people who came to talk to me wanted to know the other differences between our weddings and their own. You know I like to chat, but that day it was too much for me – having to repeat myself so many times. I had never been so happy to put my back on the bed as I was that night.'

'Cobs, you missed your calling,' Gertrude laughed. 'You would have been a first-class reporter; you told me everything I wanted to know and more. Let me just go and peep at Abu, then we can have another cup of tea…'

'No-o, I can't stay,' Cobola told her. 'Sheku has to take me home then go all the way to Kissy Road to pick up Adora.'

She had barely entered the car when Sheku's mobile rang. It was an anxious Ida calling to say the baby was coming. Torn between his duties and concern for his wife, Sheku turned to Cobola.

'Madam, what am I to do?'

'Call her number again and give me the phone,' Cobola said, and when he did as told, asked Ida how many minutes passed between each pain.

'Nanna, I'm not sure,' she panted, panic-stricken. 'Maybe fifteen …Another one is coming – ooooooh...'

Cobola waited for her to stop wailing, before saying in her calmest voice,

'Don't be afraid, ya? The first baby takes a long time to come out, believe me…Even if water starts running down your legs, that doesn't mean the baby is coming out, you hear?'

'Yes, Nanna.'

'Now go and drink some water and walk around till the next pain starts. Sheku will soon be there.'

'Yes, Nanna.'

'Alright, Sheku,' Cobola said, handing him the phone. 'Drop me at the house, then take the car to Mr. Yao's office. I'll call him right now to tell him what is happening. He will arrange for someone else to bring Adora home, so you can go and look after your wife.'

A deep sigh conveyed Sheku's relief.

'Thank you, madam,' he said, and started the car.

Cobola clicked on Yao's number but received a message that his phone was switched off. He's probably at a meeting, she said to herself and sent him a text message instead.

'Sheku,' she said, 'how did we manage without these mobile phones…eh?'

A half-suppressed chuckle from the driver's seat was the only indication that Sheku had heard her.

# EIGHT

Cobola always enjoyed sitting out on her veranda. Sometimes she went there early in the morning and listened to the local announcements and obituaries on the radio while sipping her first cup of tea. Later in the day, she would go to watch the trawlers berthed in the blue waters of White Man's Bay, and the crows and pigeons wheeling in the sky or fluttering around seeking food or straw for their nests. On some days there might be vultures as well, suggesting that preparations were being made in the neighbourhood for a ritual feast for the dead. Whenever a pair of birds settled close together on a telephone wire, she always thought of them as having a cozy chat, such as she had so often enjoyed with her late husband and still did with Gertrude. That was where she was on the Saturday morning when Yao called her mobile to say he was on his way

'I told Adora to leave the door open for you,' Cobola said. 'Walk right in and come out to the veranda.'

He arrived two minutes later, bearing a gift from Isabella of a small Madeira cake.

'Bella is so sweet!' Cobola exclaimed as he kissed her. 'You people are spoiling me-o.'

'This one is for a particular reason, Nanna,' Yao said. 'Bella reminded me that Monday will make it one year and a day since you came to live with us.'

'One year already, eh! It's true what they say: time flies when you're enjoying yourself.'

'So, I take it, you have no regrets.'

'None whatsoever, my dear; I didn't know what I was missing. Living so close to you both and to my grandchildren is a big, big blessing. These days I look forward to waking up in the morning.'

'That makes me *so* happy, Nanna, ' Yao said, grinning. 'I'm even happier because you and Bella get on well these days.'

'So am I. It wouldn't have been so nice if we weren't friends…Any news from Sheku?'

Yao slapped his forehead, chastising himself for not putting first things first.

'He phoned around seven o'clock this morning. You have another granddaughter.'

'A baby girl; how nice,' Cobola said. 'Let me talk to Sheku straightaway.'

Sheku acknowledged her congratulations, but gave only his usual two-word answers to her eager comments and questions about Ida and the new baby. In the end, admitting defeat, Cobola repeated her gratitude to the Almighty for Ida's safe delivery, sent her a message of goodwill, and clicked off.

'I still wonder how that boy managed to get Ida interested in him,' she said, shaking her head in frustration. 'He has no conversation whatsoever.'

'But, Nanna, you know he can talk when he wants to,' Yao laughed. 'He probably believes in rank and doesn't think it's proper for him to chat with you.'

'For Ida's sake I hope you are right, otherwise she must be having a very boring time with him. Anyway, that's her business…Tell me about the trouble at work.'

'As Bella said, it was much ado about nothing; just that your son was suspected of nepotism.'

'Nepotism! You? What happened?'

Instead of a direct answer, Yao asked her when last she had heard from Josiah. Josiah was the son of one of her husband's relations and had joined the Ennison household as a companion for Yao when it was certain that he was going to remain an only child. He stayed with them till he finished school and eventually found a job in one of the banks. Up till 1992, Sierra Leoneans needed no visa to enter Britain. In the late 1980s, Josiah saved enough money to spend his annual leave in England, since it fell in the rainy season, when it was summer over there. He had never returned.

'November twenty-eight to be exact', Cobola answered. 'He phoned on my birthday as usual. Why? Did the trouble have something to do with him?'

'Indirectly. Did he ever tell you that his wife already had a child when he married her?'

Cobola shook her head.

'Well, she did; a son. She had left him with her mother when she went to do nursing, and the boy was still here when she and Josiah got together. She eventually applied for a visa for him, not knowing that the British equivalent of our Ministry of the Interior had it on record that she had entered the country as a student and never left – those people are thorough-o. The visa was refused, so the boy was stranded here. Josiah only told me about it three years ago. He said he had asked the boy – he's called Sammy – to come and introduce himself to me. After that, Sammy used to drop in to see me at the office now and then.'

'I can already see where this is going,' Cobola said.

'Yes. His parents supported him financially, and he completed a course at IPAM.'

'What's IPAM?' Cobola asked.

'Oh. The Institute of Public Administration and Management, Nanna. It's on Tower Hill – near the British Council...After IPAM, Sammy worked in the civil service for a couple of years, but he wanted to leave – poor salary, mainly – the same reasons Bella resigned. When a vacancy occurred in the office, I didn't make him any promises-o, but I encouraged him to apply, and this is where the thing becomes complicated. First of all, I have to bore you with details about how we recruit staff. I'm sure you've seen adverts for jobs in the papers. In our case, people interested have to apply in writing with copies of their certificates, job experience, references, et cetera, against a certain deadline. I give one of my assistants the task of opening a file for the job in question and he or she records all the applications and the dates they were received. After the deadline, all the applications come to me. I go through them and select five or six of the best ones. When it's a fairly junior position, only heads of departments meet to conduct interviews – not the Managing Director. Sammy made the short list and performed well at the interview. His spoken English is good; so is his written English, and he had the right experience, good references, et cetera. *I* thought he was the best candidate and my opinion carried more weight because the job was in my department....The *one* mistake I made, Nanna, was not telling him to take his application to the reception desk in the first place and let them send it up. He gave it to me and, without thinking, I asked my secretary to pass on to the person compiling the applicants' file. When Sammy got the job, she remembered that he used to come to see me, that I gave her the application personally, put two and two together and made six.'

Cobola had followed Yao's account closely. She said,

'But even if your secretary suspected something, how did your boss get involved?'

'Big offices are always full of rumours, Nanna...'

'Yes-o. That is one reason I was glad your father and I were independent.'

'You were lucky. My secretary must have mentioned it to someone, who mentioned it to someone else, and so on till it got to the boss. He's always concerned about the good name of the company and not putting square pegs in round holes, so he called me to his office. Fortunately for me, I always make notes against the applicants I reject and we keep the files for some time. I assured him that I hadn't put pressure on any of the other members of the selection committee to give Sammy the job. What upset me was that he didn't take my word for it; he went and asked the others if what I had said was true... All this happened just the day before you arrived and I was still upset, which is probably why you thought I looked pulled down. Once he was satisfied that no nepotism had taken place, he sent out a circular memo about not spreading false rumours that could damage the company's good name...I gave my secretary a tongue-lashing she won't forget in a hurry. I knew *she* started it.'

'You have to be very careful in your position, eh?'

'All the time, Nanna. In fact, I'm getting tired of it. I want to leave and start my own business.'

'*Enh*! What kind of business?'

'Running a petrol station…or anything else that pays well.'

' And what does Bella say?'

'That it's a good idea but we should wait till we've reduced the debt on the house to a more manageable level.'

'That's sensible. Meanwhile you can make up your mind about what business you want to do. When you are ready you can use more of the land Auntie Aina left you to raise some cash, and I will sell my house at George Town. That should give you enough capital to start…'

'You are willing to sell the house for me, Nanna?'

'*Of course* I am. Your happiness is more important to me.'

Yao stared at her for several moments before murmuring, 'My mother'. His tenderness touched Cobola deeply but, as was usual with her, she made light of the moment by saying in a singsong voice,

'That's what mothers are for,' before going on to inquire about the rest of the family.

'Bella has gone to her tailor, Adora has gone for her singing lesson, the boys have gone to their barber, and Khadi is cooking our lunch.'

'So what are you going to do now?'

'Just relax, Nanna. It's too early to drink beer, so I'm going to have another cup of coffee and listen to one of the CDs Orlando sent for me. After lunch I'll go and play tennis, that is, unless you want me to take you to see Ida.'

'No, my dear, seeing Ida can wait; you go for your exercise. You need it,' she added, poking his abdomen. 'Your belly has begun to show.'

'What do you expect, Nanna? I'm nearly fifty, you know…'

'Of course, I know. Wasn't I there?… Anyway, age has nothing to do with it,' she went on as Yao laughed with her. 'It's all that beer…'

'Nanna, I beg to differ. Some of the biggest beer guzzlers in this town are as flat as planks. In any case, if I were going to get a pot-belly from drinking beer, I would have had one by now. Pops never got one, and he, too, liked his beer…'

'That is true; perhaps it's all a matter of luck,' Cobola conceded. 'But anyway, exercise is good.'

'And what are *you* going to do?' Yao asked.

'Me? I'll carry on enjoying the view. If I start to feel sleepy, I might go and lie on the couch for a while, or else I'll nod off right here.'

'Don't fall off your chair-o,' Yao said, as he bent to kiss her.

'Cheeky boy. I'm not that decrepit yet,' Cobola retorted as she kissed him back.

Yao played tennis with friends at the university courts on Mount Aureol. Having lost a three-set match, he decided to head for home, and was enjoying his new Jonathan Butler CD, when, just by the lower faculty flats, he saw three young people – a girl and two boys – walking down the steep road.

'Need a lift?' he called out as he always did, remembering what a trek it was to the bottom of the hill from the student hostels.

They accepted the offer gratefully, the girl taking the front seat and the boys the back.

'How far?' Yao asked.

The young men said they would get off at the Model School/Circular Road junction, but the girl told him she lived at Water Street, near Congo Cross.

'Then, you are lucky,' Yao smiled. 'That's on my way home.'

A dark-skinned beauty, not unlike Isabella when he first set eyes on her, the girl responded with a dimpled smile so charming that he had to remind himself that he was middle-aged, and married.

'Presumably all of you are students?' he asked, assuming a fatherly air.

One of the young men spoke for them all.

'Yes, sir.'

'And how is Fourah Bay College these days?'.

'Not at all good, sir,' the other one said. 'The lecturers are threatening to go on strike because of conditions of service, all the buildings are falling to pieces, most of the library books are out of date, we have no bookshop, and the food they give us is rubbish.'

'Only fit for jailbirds,' the first one added.

'It's a reflection of the current state of our country,' Yao said. 'Not that it was ever like home cooking but, in my day, most of the time the food wasn't bad at all, neither was the library; and the bookshop was *great...*'

The young men expressed astonishment that the life of a student had once been so pleasant, but the girl seemed more interested in the fact that Yao was an FBC graduate than in the deterioration of the college.'

'Oh, yes,' he said when she asked. '1979 to 1982. I once knew every corner of this campus.'

They parted company with the young men at the bottom of the hill, by which time Yao had discovered that all three were accountancy students hoping to enter the business world on graduation.

Alone with him, the girl said, 'I'm Miriam… And you?'

Somewhat taken aback by her forwardness, Yao answered,

'Oh. Ennison.'

She flashed him another dimpled smile.

'Pleased to meet you.'

Unlike the young men, she hadn't once addressed him as 'sir', which Yao thought disrespectful, considering the huge difference in their ages; but he continued to make affable small talk as they headed west. They were approaching the Peace Bridge when she said coyly, 'I like your music-o.'

'Thank you.' Yao said.

To his astonishment, she went on, 'And I like you; won't you take me for a drive? It's been a long time since I saw Lumley Beach.'

Before he could think of a suitable answer, she had put out her hand and stroked his bare knee, making it necessary for him to correct a swerve. Ah-ah, he said to himself. It was disturbing enough that the girl seemed to be trying to seduce him, but even more so that he felt a throb in his crotch. Removing her hand and placing it firmly on her lap helped him regain control of himself then, thinking quickly, he decided that instead of giving the little Jezebel the telling-off she deserved, he would ignore her brazen overture. It was, therefore, with paternal gallantry that he said,

'My dear, it would have been a pleasure to take you to the beach, but I need a shower, and my wife and I always eat together in the evening.'

Out of the corner of his eye, he saw the girl's mouth open and close. But recovering fast, she said, 'Perhaps another time?'

'I don't think so-o,' Yao chuckled. 'And let me give you some free advice... ya? Don't waste yourself on old men like me. You have beauty, and above average intelligence otherwise you wouldn't be at FBC. If you get a good degree in accountancy your future will be bright – even in this country. Just work hard and be patient.'

'Thank you, sir,' the girl said, but she sounded more amused than impressed, and gave Yao a look suggesting that he didn't know what he was talking about. Not long afterwards, they arrived at the Water Street junction and he stopped to let her out. As she opened the door to depart, she said,

'Goodbye, sir. And thank you for the lift.'

Two 'sirs' in less than two minutes, Yao thought with satisfaction. He was pleased with the way he'd handled the situation though, from her attitude, he doubted that the girl would heed his advice. Instant gratification seemed to be the order of the day in the city, particularly among young people. It was as if the corruption they heard about all the time, and the profusion of mansions on the hills, and of four-wheel drive vehicles in the narrow, chewed-up streets, had convinced them that only fools tried to secure their future through hard work and perseverance. All he could do was try to influence his own children and any other young people who came within his orbit.

He felt even more pleased with himself when, just as he turned into the road to Murray Town, he heard shouts of 'Daddy!' and saw the twins sprinting towards him from Wilkinson Road. They climbed into the car, mingling their sweaty smell with his.

'Where are you coming from?' he asked.

'The beach. We were playing volley ball with some Lebanese boys.'

Yao clasped his hands over the steering wheel for a moment, silently giving thanks that he hadn't put himself in the position of perhaps having to explain to Isabella's sons what he was doing with a young woman, more than half his age, and who was no relation of theirs. But the incident, with its unexplored possibilities, stayed on his mind all evening, so that when they retired for the night he grabbed Isabella from behind, kissing her neck and shoulders as eagerly as if they'd been married for a few hours instead of nearly twenty years. Isabella, who was applying a night cream to her face and thinking about her upcoming check-up, protested a little; but Yao persisted, and since she had by now come to terms with her disfigurement, the thought that he still hungered for her scarred and aging body gave her such joy that she leaned back against him and wiped off the residue of cream in a hurry.

They pleasured each other to their bodies' content, then lay in a languid tangle of arms and legs till Yao murmured, 'Babes, I need a glass of water. How about you?'

'Yes, please – a big one.'

While she was waiting, Isabella pulled herself up against the bed head. Yao joined her a few minutes later and they chatted as they drank, relishing the perfect moment – that was until Yao tossed a pebble into the pool of their contentment.

'Let me tell you what happened when I was coming home from tennis this evening,' he said. 'I gave a girl a lift – an FBC student... Babes, she came on to me-o – *big* time – even suggested that I should drive her to Lumley Beach...'

99

To his consternation Isabella jabbed his side with her elbow and put more space between them.

'So *that* was why you pounced on me like that,' she said with indignation, 'You were thinking about *her...*'

Of course, there was some truth in that accusation, but not enough for Yao to feel guilty as he assured Isabella that not only did she make it impossible for another woman to cross his mind while they were making love, but also that the girl hadn't interested him in the least.

'I only mentioned her because of her shocking behaviour.'

'Liar,' Isabella said, but her voice had lost its accusatory edge and she didn't resist when he pulled her back to him.

'At least, you were not foolish enough to take her to the beach; she must have been angling for a handout.'

'Babes, how do you know?' Yao asked, and went on with playful suggestiveness. 'Perhaps she fell for me in my white polo and shorts.'

Isabella sucked her teeth. 'More likely, she'd fallen for your Volvo. I don't think a nice body counts when girls are looking for sugar daddies-o.'

'Well, had I encouraged her, she would soon have found out that Ennison isn't a catch where money is concerned.'

'Don't I know that!' Isabella joked and they laughed comfortably together. Not long afterwards they kissed good night and settled down to sleep, but a couple of hours later, Isabella's mobile trilled on her bedside cabinet forcing her, moaning, to open her eyes.

Speaking in a low voice, Cobola said, 'You all come-o, Adora is sick. '

Wide awake in an instant, Isabella flung off her cover and gave Yao a vigorous shake.

'Wake up. Wake up. Nanna says Adora is sick.'

She was hurrying along the dark corridor, barefooted, before Yao could collect himself. Already dressed to go out, Cobola met her at the door and said in the same low voice, 'She has vomited twice, and I don't think it's malaria because she is moaning a bit and complaining of pain here.' She pointed to a spot below her navel on the right side. 'Let's take her to hospital straightaway. It might be her appendix.'

Yao, who joined them just then, asked, 'Which hospital; Connaught?'

'Choithram,' Isabella answered in her decisive way. 'Connaught is closer, but I'm not sure about the emergency services at night.'

'Alright, I'll be back,' Yao said.

Having dressed in a hurry, he returned with his car keys and a torch which he handed to Cobola before scooping up Adora who was curled up on her grandmother's bed.

'Hush, ya, sweetheart,' he murmured. Adora draped one slender arm around his neck and answered in a small voice, 'Yes, Daddy.' Yao held her closer.

'Let me get some shawls; that place is cold,' Cobola said as he headed for the door. Isabella, meanwhile, had left them to put on trousers and a T-shirt and tell the boys what was happening.

The long drive up to Hill Station seemed to take forever, especially when, after another bout of retching, Adora complained more insistently of pain. Isabella became so anxious that even before Yao pulled up his handbrake in the hospital's grounds, she had opened the door and dashed inside the building to fetch an orderly with a trolley. It took only a brief consultation and examination for the young Indian doctor on emergency duty to have Adora whisked into the theatre.

Isabella stroked Cobola's hand while they waited for news.

'Nanna, thank you,' she said. 'We might have kept her at home till morning because she always moans like that when she has been vomiting.'

'Don't forget I was a nurse-o,' Cobola said. 'You don't joke with pain in that place.'

Once the surgeon had assured them that Adora had gone through the operation well and was no longer in any danger, she said to Isabella,

'No doubt you are staying.'

'Yes, Nanna.'

Cobola would have liked to stay herself, but since Isabella didn't suggest it, she handed her the shawls. However, hoping to leave Adora awake, she lingered in the ward while Isabella accompanied Yao to the car. Adora's eyelids fluttered, but her eyes remained closed. After another couple of minutes, Cobola kissed her forehead and hurried after her parents.

Yao had put his arm around Isabella's waist as they strolled towards his car.

'Babes, I wish I could stay.'

'Me, too; but apart from taking Nanna home, you need more sleep after so much activity yesterday…'

'*You* were pretty active yourself,' he murmured in her ear.

Isabella shrugged him away.

'I wasn't talking about that; I was talking about playing tennis…and fighting temptation…'

Cobola didn't hear this conversation but their body language made her smile and move ahead of them, saying over her shoulder as she passed, 'Lovebirds.'

Quite early the next morning Isabella received two phone calls in quick succession; the first from her mother-in-law and the second from her husband, both asking how the rest of the night had been.

'Very quiet, Nanna,' she told Cobola. 'Adora woke up once with little moans, but the nurse gave her an injection and she went straight back to sleep. She's still sleeping.'

'No fever?'

'No fever. They put her on an antibiotic drip as well.'

'Good. Yao will bring me up to relieve you just now, and I will phone Khadi to tell her to be prepared to spend the night at the hospital so you can rest for work tomorrow...'

'Thank you, Nanna,' Isabella said, but when Yao called, she remarked with amusement, 'Yao, you say I like to organise people? Nanna takes first prize.'

'No comment,' he answered, with a chuckle; but in front of the bathroom mirror, shaving, he thought contentedly: what a difference a change of circumstances can make. Ten years ago Bella would have said, *"That your mother...* She wants to take over my family."

Adora spent only two days in hospital, but the surgeon instructed that she rest at home till her wound was completely healed and the clips removed.

This meant that while Isabella was in Accra for her check-up, Cobola had her all to herself. They were sitting together on the couch a few days after her discharge when Cobola said,

'Darling, we've hardly had time to talk since I came back. Tell me about Ballanta Academy. Do you like it?'

'Yes, Nanna, but sometimes the lessons are boring. Our teacher makes us go over and over the same things. She says they have to become habits.'

All of a sudden, Adora sprang to her feet. 'We have to stand up straight like this, and put one leg in front of the other before we start to sing.'

She made her grandmother laugh out loud by holding the pose, then alarmed her by stretching her neck and starting to sing a scale.

'Darling, leave the rest of the demonstration till your clips are out, ya?' Cobola said, flapping her hand to stop her, 'Sit down again and tell me more.'

'I have to practise breathing from my diaphragm, so that the veins in my neck don't show when I'm singing...My teacher says the sound has to come from here.'

Adora bunched her fingers together, pointing at her forehead.

'*Enh*!' Cobola said, 'I never knew there was so much to learn about singing. I thought it all came naturally.'

'And we have to learn how to read music too, and how to pronounce words clearly. The whole class takes nearly three hours.'

'And you sing songs, I hope, not only scales?'

'Yes, Nanna. I'm learning a new one right now – classical, then we are going to learn jazz, pop, spirituals and gospel...'

'*Enh*! And how many of you are in the class?'

'Only four of us. Two girls and two boys...'

'You like them?'

'Yes, Nanna, especially a girl called Theresa Banya, and a boy called Chimah Cummings...He is one year younger that Eric and Derek and sings in the choir at Holy Trinity. He can play the guitar well.'

'*Enh*,' Cobola said.

There was something about Adora's voice and manner that made Cobola suspect that she had become a bit infatuated with the boy called Chimah. The thought crossed her mind then that in another year or two Adora might start causing them anxious moments. Always a pretty girl, she was fast becoming the kind of curvy beauty that reminded Cobola of herself at that age.

It was during Adora's convalescence, that Cobola realised that Kweku was no longer the first thing on her mind when she woke up in the morning, or the last thing on it before she fell asleep at night.'

'Thank God!' Gertrude said when she confided in her. 'You have mourned for that man long enough. Life is for the living.'

'I know, Trudy; but I didn't think I would ever feel this way.' Cobola answered. ' I don't even feel the need to go to the cemetery to tell Kweku things now.'

'Thank God!' Gertrude said again. Baptized and confirmed a Methodist, she had become a Jehovah's Witness when she married Abu and, as a result, had long abandoned all traditional practices connected with the dead. 'As I kept telling you,' she went on, 'apart from when you had to pay that man who looks after Kweku's grave, you didn't have to strain yourself going to that rugged place. The dead are dead. They don't hear anything.'

Cobola had no evidence to the contrary, but it had always comforted her to think that the dead continued to interact with the living somehow, and she could have sworn that there had often been a loving presence when she stood beside Kweku's grave. What seemed to have happened slowly but surely was that as she became more involved with Yao's family, the chapter of her life involving Kweku Ennison, beautiful as it had been, had finally closed. Once again her identity had changed, she now realised. She had become Nanna; even to Orlando and Beverly. Ah, well, she said to herself perhaps, to

107

enjoy life to the full, you have keep leaving the past behind; and life itself helps you to do that unless *you* prevent it. All the same, for a while she felt a little disloyal.

Once again Isabella returned from Ghana with the assurance that she was perfectly healthy, and Abu, whom Cobola had thought about to pass through the final curtain, recovered enough to walk out to his veranda, albeit slowly and always in pyjamas. He spent a few hours there every morning, reading his newspapers, and *Watchtower* magazine, listening to the BBC World Service, or chatting with his visitors. No other dramas disturbed the even tenor of Cobola's days and, before she realised it, another year was over.

The Volvo could only accommodate four passengers and she had already made it clear that she considered it much more important for the younger Ennisons to be sitting on the same pew during the watch night service than for her to be in church herself so, since Khadi always spent new year's eve and new year's day with her own family, she was alone when 2008 drew to a close.

She passed the hours before midnight nodding in front of the television, but came fully awake as the countdown to 2009 began. The moment the televised gong fell silent, she struggled to her feet and raised her eyes and arms to thank God for allowing her to see in another year then, knowing that the rest of the family would return within the hour, she put the pot of pepper soup Khadi had prepared earlier on low heat and laid out bowls and spoons ready for the family tradition of having a bowl of soup together to start the year. She was still pottering around in the kitchen when she heard Adora's joyful voice calling,

'Nanna, happy new year!'

'Happy new year! Happy new year!' Cobola sang out and met them at the door with open arms. She exchanged hugs, kisses and more loving wishes with each member of the family thinking, as she did so: Cobola Ennison, you are truly, truly blessed.

# NINE

Abu Kargbo slipped away without warning towards the end of the next rainy season. There had been a terrific storm the night before, with thunder crashing loudly enough for Cobola to have to cover her ears with her pillow. The bright, fresh-smelling morning that followed the storm had drawn her to the veranda. Soil washed into the bay from the surrounding hills had temporarily turned its waters a dingy reddish colour, but she still decided to have her breakfast outside and was there, relishing being alive and reasonably healthy, when her mobile interrupted her peace. It was Gertrude.

In a flat voice, and without preliminaries, she said,

'Cobs, I beg you. Come. Abu died just now.'

'Ay, ya!' Cobola cried, ' I'm coming.'

Her heart skipped and raced as she told Ida the news and asked her to go to the main road for a taxi, since Yao and Isabella had already left for work.

'Leave my namesake with Khadi so you can go faster,' she said. 'And if the taxi driver refuses to come, tell him I will pay for one hour.'

The young people were still on vacation and yet to emerge from their rooms. Deciding that there was no reason to rouse them, she steadied herself with a prayer, then spent a few minutes deciding what to pack, since there was no question of her not staying with Gertrude for a while. Her next action was to send text messages to Yao and Isabella who sent messages back sympathising and saying they would see her at the Kargbos' in the evening.

The front door was wide open when Cobola arrived at Gertrude's house, and she walked straight in – right up to Gertrude who was talking to two of her neighbours. Gertrude rose at once to greet her and, as they held each other close, let out a couple of deep sobs. That, Cobola discovered, would be the extent of her friend's public grieving, even when Abu's female relations arrived and wailed on her shoulders.

'My sister, come and sit down,' Gertrude said. 'I was just telling them what happened...I helped Abu with his bath and breakfast and he went out to the veranda as usual. While I was having my own bath, one of his younger friends, Festus Bangura, came to see him and found him sitting like an empty bag, with his chin on his chest. At first Festus thought Abu had fallen asleep, but he had gone – just like that.'

As her listeners commiserated with her, Gertrude asked to be excused and gave Cobola's skirt a tug, signalling her to follow. Outside the sitting-room, she whispered, 'Cobs, I want you to do me a big, big favour.'

'Trudy, anything,' Cobola answered, and was only slightly dismayed when Gertrude said, 'I want you to help me wash Abu before the funeral home people come to take him away. You think you can manage? We'll do it slowly.'

'Trudy, it will be an honour to help you,' Cobola said. 'I will manage.'

'I knew this day was coming soon,' Gertrude explained when Cobola expressed surprise at seeing two pairs of surgical gloves and clean bed sheets as well as other items they needed. 'I had been praying for it to happen here and not in hospital. I wanted to do this last thing for Abu.'

'Always so practical,' Cobola murmured. 'Has the doctor come yet?'

'Yes, he passed by on the way to his surgery. Festus went with him to collect the death certificate for me, and to contact the funeral home.'

Weeping quietly, Sia brought in buckets of warm water and, as instructed, remained just outside the door while the two old friends bent their backs to the task of giving Abu a bed bath the way they had been taught as nurses in training. Gertrude shed a few tears as she wiped Abu's peaceful face, and crooned a funeral hymn in a shaky voice:

*'Sleep on, beloved, sleep and take thy rest.*
*Lay down thy head upon the Saviour's breast.*
*We love thee well, but Jesus loves thee best,*
*Good night, good night, good night.*

Cobola had tried to join in, but the moment she opened her own mouth, a painful spasm closed her throat and she could only hum. They wrapped Abu's body in one of the clean sheets and Sia cleared away the soiled things. Then Gertrude surprised Cobola again because, in spite of her past insistence that the dead heard nothing, dry-eyed now, and her voice steady, she addressed the motionless form:

'Abu Kargbo, I don't want anything to disturb my peace of mind in the coming days, so I want to say something before your body leaves this house…I don't like what you did-o, dying behind my back like that. Giving me such a shock. I deserved better treatment from you after all these years. I was a good wife to you and I never looked at another man – not even when you gave me good cause to. And I gave you sons as well as a daughter. You should not have left me without saying goodbye... Anyway, you, too, were a good husband on the whole, and a very good father, so I won't complain anymore. And I will mourn for you. But let me tell you at once. I won't be like Cobola-o, mourning for years and years. As long as I'm well, I'm going to *enjoy* my life till my own time comes. *Lonta.*'

She stood in silence for a moment then, muttering, 'Hm. Abu Kargbo, a corpse', turned away with a shrug. Cobola's cheeks were wet, but amusement mingled with her sadness. Shaking her head, she said to herself: Gertrude is a case.

While they rested between callers, Gertrude said to her, 'I see you came prepared to stay.'

'Yes. I'm staying till Judith comes. And I'm sleeping with *you.*'

'Thank you, my dear sister,' Gertrude said, 'but let me warn you: I fart at night-o – like a bugle. Abu used to complain, and even threatened to move to another room – as if *he* didn't do it too.'

'Exactly,' Cobola laughed. 'We'll blast on each other. When are you expecting the children?'

'In a few days; but only Judith and young Abu. Eddie says he doesn't have a green card yet and that if he leaves the States they won't let him in again.'

'Ah, this immigration business,' Cobola sighed, 'Perhaps, he should find an American girl to marry like some people do...Anyway, two out of three children at their father's funeral is still good.'

Those few days dragged. Relations from both sides of Gertrude's family took up temporary residence at the Wilkinson Road house, leaving just one small room left for young Abu. Food preparation seemed to go on throughout the day, amid loud conversations, and sympathisers streamed in and out from morning till night. In the end, it all became too much for Cobola so that, even though she wanted to give Gertrude her full support, she was relieved when Judith and young Abu arrived and she could escape to the peace and quiet of her own home in the evenings.

'My feet missed you-o,' she told Adora on her first evening back. ' Am I going to get a rub?'

'Yes, Nanna – and hair brushing too, if you want it.'

'Darling, God will bless you. I will sleep like my namesake tonight,' Cobola said, and settled down to enjoy being pampered.

The school vacation ended a few days later and Adora moved up to the first of the senior classes. This meant that she now attended the afternoon shift and had to find her way home by public transport, rarely arriving before dark. Apart from having to do without her late evening foot rub during the week, Cobola hated the idea of school girls being out in the streets that late.

'It's not right,' she complained to Gertrude sometime after Abu's funeral. 'Had she been my daughter, and I could afford it, I would have moved her to a private school.'

'Well, she's not your daughter,' Gertrude said, 'And I hope you are not going to tell her parents what you think.'

'No-o; I know my place. I'll just continue to pray, and keep telling her to be careful.'

'That's all that you can do, my dear sister. She has to learn how to cope with life in present-day Freetown. She's old enough.'

Cobola didn't think so, and continued to fret over the situation. She brought up subject again, and on that occasion, told Gertrude how much she wished Adora lived in a country with enough secondary schools to accommodate all pupils in single sessions as it had been in their day, and for so many years after independence.

'And don't tell me it was the war, Trudy.'

Gertrude wasn't about to say anything of the sort. Missing Abu's grumpy presence far more than she had expected to, and still not fully recovered from the upheaval caused by his death and the stress of his funeral, she had temporarily lost her zest for living and the things that went with that, such as taking pleasure in good food and in her chats with Cobola. All she said was,

'My sister, put your mind at rest…ya? The child will be all right. Are you not the one always telling people God is good?'

'Yes-o,' Cobola answered. 'Thanks for reminding me.'

Nevertheless, she didn't relax after dark till Adora said,

'Good evening, Nanna.'

# TEN

The twins had begun their medical studies that October and now lived in a hostel at COMAHS's Kossoh Town campus. It was ten miles to the east of Freetown, so that their grandmother saw even less of them than before. She was therefore delighted when they knocked on her door on a Saturday afternoon in December. They had started their Christmas vacation the previous day but had arrived too late in the evening for anything more than a quick greeting.

'Don't they feed you in that place?' Cobola asked as soon as they had hugged and kissed her again. 'You both look as if you've lost at least five pounds, and it's not just because you've grown.'

'The food is not too bad, Nanna,' Eric said, 'even though it's not like what Mummy and Khadi cook. It's the course that is making us lose weight... It's *hard.* '

'And to think you have nearly six more years of it,' Cobola said. 'At this rate, there won't be any flesh on your bones when you graduate.'

She couldn't have been more surprised when, as they laughed away her fears, Derek said, 'Nanna, we'll survive – in the mighty name of Jesus.'

Since no one in their household was given to such utterances, Cobola exclaimed, 'Ay-ay, you boys are born-again now?'

'Yes, Nanna,' Eric answered with a broad smile. 'We go to an Assemblies of God church at Kossoh Town and have accepted Jesus as our lord and personal saviour. We've even been baptized by the Holy Spirit...'

Cobola's wide eyes opened wider.

'You mean you speak in tongues ?'

'Yes, Nanna, and next term we are going to be baptized like Jesus.'

'Covering all your body with water.'

'Yes, Nanna,' Eric said, still beaming.'

'I see. Do your parents know?'

'Yes, Nanna,' Derek said. 'Mummy says she wants to hear more about it and that she'll come to church with us one Sunday while we are here, but Daddy is very annoyed. He says that is not what he sent us to college for, and that we have already been baptized and confirmed as Christians.'

'And Adora?'

'She knows; but Daddy says she's going to be confirmed as an Anglican and we are not to confuse her.' He added with a shrug, 'We have to obey him...'

'Of course you do,' Cobola said. 'And what are you going to do about church while you are home? You know Daddy likes you all to go the Cathedral with him.'

'We 'll go with him, Nanna; but if there is any Sunday that he doesn't go to church, we'll go to our own. The headquarters are not far from here.'

'Hmm,' Cobola said, 'Well, I can only pray that you'll be happy in your faith, and that Daddy comes round.'

'Thank you, Nanna,' they said solemnly, speaking together as they often did. A pause followed, during which Cobola invited them to help themselves to soft drinks and Isabella's latest Madeira cake.

Eric said, 'Nanna?...' then hesitated as if afraid his grandmother might think him disrespectful. Having a good idea what was on his mind, Cobola said,

'You want to know if *I* have accepted Jesus as my lord and savior, eh?'

'Yes, Nanna.'

'If you mean have I ever gone forward at a crusade or in a church, then my answer has to be no; but Jesus is my *person-o*. Nowadays I feel almost as close to him as I do to God.'

'Nanna,' Eric said, 'God and Jesus are the same.'

When she told the twins that she didn't subscribe to that doctrine, their troubled expressions made her smile,

'Don't worry about me...ya?' she said. 'As I told you, God and I are close. We've been close for more than fifty years – *very* close for the last ten years. I even quarrel with Him sometimes; that should tell you how close we are.'

The brothers looked even more dismayed, as if they were now certain that their beloved Nanna was on the road to perdition. Derek said,

'Nanna, you quarrel with God?'

Cobola answered serenely,

'Okay, not quarrel – complain...Yes, I complain when He lets bad things happen – especially when they happen to good people. I've told you we are close.

Eric wanted to know if God ever answered her.

'Yes, darling. Sometimes he tells me that I should keep quiet and trust him. At other times he puts me in my place the way he put Job in his place. Do you know that story?'

'Not the part where God put him in his place...'

'Okay. Now that you read your Bibles every day – born-again people have to do that, yes?'

They confirmed it with smiles, and she went on, 'I'm giving the two of you homework. Read Job. You'll see how God put him in his place. If you like, we can talk about it next time you come, but now, I want to hear about COMAHS. I hope your lecturers are making the courses interesting.'

'Yes, Nanna; most of them try,' Eric said.

For the next hour, the twins entertained her with accounts of the peculiarities of their tutors and other campus characters. Some of their stories sent her into peals of laughter so that when they made a move to leave, she said,

'Come and visit me again-o. Next time I want to hear more about your social life.'

'Nanna, if you mean girlfriends, there is nothing to tell,' Eric answered, laughing. 'Between our lectures, studying, and church activities, we don't have time for that.'

'But we have friends who are girls,' Derek told her.

'Anyway,' Cobola said, 'I still want at least one more visit, you hear?.'

The next day, it was Yao who visited her. It happened during the interval between the family's return from church and Sunday lunch, which she always had with them. Cobola had already decided that she would let *him* raise the sensitive subject of the twins' decision to join a charismatic church, and didn't have long to wait. Yao had hardly sat down when he said,

'Nanna, I'm upset…' And indeed, she hadn't seen him so grim-faced since the day he told her about Isabella's illness.

'When you've just come from church?' Cobola answered lightly, 'That isn't a good advertisement for Christianity. You should be feeling and looking uplifted.'

'Well I'm not,' Yao said flatly. 'In a way, it's the very Christianity that has upset me – at least, one version of it…Your grandsons have started going to one of those clapping, dancing, speaking-in-tongues churches at Kossoh Town. They say they've been born again…'

'Yes, they told me. But why should that upset you, Yao? They are worshipping the same God, only in a different way.'

'Nanna, Ennisons are Anglicans,' Yao answered in a stubborn tone. 'Pops sang in the choir at the Cathedral most of his life. Grandma Dora was active in church associations in her day, and so were you. *I* am a sidesman…I expect my sons to keep up the family tradition…'

'But, Yao, you should know by now that children don't always follow in their parents' footsteps when they grow up…'

'Those boys are not adults,' Yao growled.

'If they are old enough to go to college and to vote, they are old enough to decide how they want to worship God,' Cobola told him gently. 'You just have to accept their decision, my dear; there's nothing you can do about that.'

Yao's expression darkened further and, in an attempt to lift his spirits, Cobola reminded him that the twins could have behaved in ways that even she would have found upsetting – like not being interested in education, or drinking and smoking, using drugs, and behaving recklessly with girls.

'They are good boys,' she said. 'You should be proud of them. And they say they'll go to church with you while they are here, if that's what you want. They went with you today, didn't they?'

Yao nodded, but continued to look as if he wanted to hit something which made Cobola suspect that his sons' defection wasn't the only reason for his displeasure. He looked away when she peered into his eyes, saying, 'Something else is worrying you,' and several moments passed before he admitted that she was right.

'Nanna, it's Bella. Ever since we got married she has complained about the Cathedral and compared it unfavourably with King Memorial, where we got married. She says Anglicans are too stiff, their hymns are too dry, their sermons too bookish, their prayers too formal, and that she only feels uplifted when we're singing psalms. '

Cobola loved the staid formality of Anglican services herself, having grown up with them, but she could well understand why they wouldn't be to everybody's taste – Gertrude for one. Ever since Kweku's funeral, Gertrude had referred to the Cathedral as, 'that your aristo church.'

'So why don't you go to King Memorial sometimes – just to please her.'

'Nanna, we've done that several times. She says King Memorial doesn't uplift her anymore – that nowadays there's too much emphasis on the collections... What is really worrying me is that of late she has been complaining more and more and I feel that the boys' decision is going to influence her. Already she is talking about going to church with them one Sunday...'

'Nothing wrong with that, or is it that you're afraid she too might become born-again?'

'Yes, Nanna. I know it will cause problems between us. Becoming born-again isn't just another way of worshipping God, as you seem to think. It's a whole way of life. Right now – by the way, I shouldn't be telling you this, so please don't say anything to Auntie Gertrude...' Cobola gave him

125

her word, and he went on, 'Right now, my senior clerk is suffering because his wife has joined one of those churches…'

'*Suffering*? Yao, that's a strong word-o.'

'That's exactly what he said, Nanna. Suffering. He says that now his wife won't drink even one glass of beer or watch DVDs with him for company's sake, and she no longer agrees to go to parties if she thinks there will be dancing. Her only subjects of conversation are domestic affairs and—what she's read in her devotional guide that day. She spends all her free time listening to gospel music and sermons on the radio, and fasts at least once a week. Sometimes, she dresses all in white and…Oh, so many complaints, Nanna. He says that when he objects to her behaviour, she tells him that obeying the word of God is all that matters to her now.'

During her thirty-plus years working as a midwife, Cobola had heard enough stories about careless and misbehaving husbands for it to cross her mind that Yao's clerk might have contributed to his wife's decision to focus on spiritual things. But confident that that didn't apply to Yao and Isabella, she kept the thought to herself.

'Poor fellow,' she said. 'That must be hard on him.'

'Nanna, he cried in my office...'

'*Enh*! Then I can understand why you're so concerned. For a man to cry in front of another man…He must be desperate.'

'He is-o.'

Wanting to help, but not knowing what else would ease Yao's troubled mind, Cobola asked him when last he prayed.

'I mean really prayed, not just a quick thank you or call for help, or those prayers we recite in church.'

Again, Yao took a while to answer. 'On the day Bella went for her operation, I got down on my knees, Nanna, but I was so scared I could only say the Lord's Prayer; and I thanked God with all my heart on the day the oncologist told us she was as certain as she could be that Bella's cancer was not as dangerous as some.'

'Which is going on for three years,' Cobola said. 'Far, from enough, my dear. Being active in the church is good, but it's not the main thing-o; the main thing is keeping close to God and obeying Him. Don't forget God was there long before people came on the scene with their many, many beliefs and religions…You need to pray more.'

For the first time since he entered the room, Yao laughed, though there wasn't much amusement in the sound.

'Nanna, what should I pray for?' he said. 'How can I ask God to act against His will when what He wants is for everybody to be born again? Isn't that what Jesus told, was it Nicodemus?'

'Yes, Nicodemus. First of all, to me, what being born-again means is deciding to trust and obey God with all your heart. That isn't something that happens naturally; you have to make up your mind to do it. Also, I'm not saying that you should beg God for any special favour. Just talk to him from your heart – the way that clerk talked to you; the way you are talking to me now. You and Bella love each other. God likes love; and he is good.'

'So you keep saying, Nanna. Sometimes I wonder if that isn't wishful thinking.'

'My dear, I've experienced God's goodness too often in my life for it to be wishful thinking. But you have to stay close to Him and obey his commandments. That's the thing.'

Before Yao could make another comment, Adora came to call them for lunch.

'Nanna, *I* cooked today, she said, with a proud smile. 'Mummy only made salad and dessert.'

'*Enh*! Then this is a *special* lunch!' Cobola answered. 'Let me go somewhere quickly so I can enjoy it all the more. You both go ahead.'

Having eaten well of the tasty meal Adora had prepared, Yao said he and Isabella were going to rest for a while. He told Eric and Derek *they* were to clear the table and clean up the kitchen because Adora and their mother had done the cooking. Since they hated housework and always tried to avoid it, Adora smirked, expecting to see long faces on her brothers. But to everyone's surprise the boys said, 'Yes, Daddy,' with saintly cheerfulness and started on their task.

Once out of the children's hearing, Cobola said, thinking to inject some humour into the situation,

'You see? Born-again sons are a good thing.'

Isabella responded with a weak smile, but Yao merely grunted, making it plain that it would take more than her mild joke to amuse him. However, he seemed in a better mood when he returned to Cobola's part of the house two hours later. The twins had gone out to meet friends and he'd come to invite her to join the rest of the family on a drive to Lumley Beach. Cobola declined the invitation, saying she couldn't be bothered to change into going out clothes. The real reason was that she thought the more time Yao and Isabella spent together, the more their marriage would withstand whatever challenges might lie ahead. She would have liked Adora to stay home with her but, of course, didn't suggest it.

As it turned out, Isabella had no opportunity to go to a different kind of service during the twins' vacation. On the three Sundays they were home, Yao attended matins at the Cathedral and, as they were expected to, his family went with him. However, the Christmas season, with its traditional psalms and English carols, kept Isabella uplifted enough not to utter one word of complaint against the Cathedral. Yao started the new year with high hopes that she'd abandoned the idea of looking for another church, but the following weeks shattered that illusion.

# ELEVEN

The thing was that Isabella had a problem, but not wanting to upset her family, she had kept it well hidden behind a show of cheerful optimism, confiding only in Ilara Rogers, her bosom friend since primary school. Ilara was the one person she had told that, while she had fully accepted losing part of her breast, she continued to have bouts of fear that the cancer would return. The weeks just before her check-ups were always the worst, and the oncologist's smiling assurances that all was well, brought her only temporary relief. Some time after her third check-up, she said to Ilara,

'I can't go on like this-o. You remember that story about the sword of Damocles? That's how I feel – as if something dangerous is hanging over my head, and it could drop on me at any time. Had I been living in UK or America, I would have gone to a therapist, but what can I do here? If I go to my doctor, he'll only put me on tranquillisers.'

'Why don't you try one of these born-again pastors?' Ilara suggested. '*I* don't know-o, but some people say their prayers work wonders.'

'Yao won't like it,' Isabella answered. 'He was *mad* when the twins told him they'd joined Assemblies of God.'

'Is he the one suffering?' Ilara asked in her challenging way.

A self-proclaimed feminist, Ilara Rogers owned a beauty salon and the popular boutique where Isabella bought some of her clothes. And she'd never married, though she had a fifteen-year-old son. Fortunately, she got on quite well with Yao, but he'd once told Isabella that no man wanting a peaceful home, would marry a woman who felt she had to assert herself all the time. 'Bella, she's tiring after a while,' he had said. Isabella could well imagine his reaction to that provocative question, but it was what gave her the impetus to seek a spiritual solution to her problem.

On the Monday following that conversation, Yao came home from work with the news that Boss Man, as he called the Managing Director, had asked him to arrange a weekend retreat for all the senior staff.

'He says he wants to make sure that we're all singing from the same hymn sheet,' he told Isabella. 'We're going to the Catholic rest house on Leicester Peak straight after work on Friday afternoon, coming back Sunday evening.'

'That's nice for you all,' Isabella said. 'Will you leave the car for me? I'll take the opportunity to go to that church up the road that the boys spoke about. Nanna might want to come…'

Yao agreed to her request with a sinking heart, and expressed his disapproval when she asked if she could take Adora with her. However, he didn't forbid it and, ignoring his attitude, she invited Cobola to join them. Cobola had only watched charismatic services on television. In the prevailing circumstances, she accepted the invitation gladly.

She was immediately struck by the joyous, welcoming atmosphere in the church, but when the pastor told the congregation to stand up and pray individually and aloud, and the buzzing of a thousand bees erupted around her, she decided that, after a lifetime of Anglican services, *she* would never be able to endure such noisy exuberance on a regular basis. Besides, though she liked one or two of the choruses, she also missed the Cathedral's majestic pipe organ, and what she considered proper hymns, with rhyming lines, connected verses and inspiring messages. Then again, the average age of the congregation seemed to be under thirty-five. Even the pastor looked as if he'd only recently graduated from Bible college, though she liked his sermon which was based on one of her favourite Bible passages: *Let not your heart be troubled. Believe in God, believe also in me.*

Adora seemed to be enjoying the experience, but it was difficult for Cobola to gauge Isabella's reaction until the pastor asked them to bow their heads for a session of intercessory prayer. Before he began to speak, the small mixed choir sang a chorus whose first line was: *Because He lives, I can face tomorrow; because he lives, all fear is gone,* and all of a sudden, Isabella began to cry. Based on her own experience, Cobola knew that women of Isabella's age were easily moved to tears, so she merely took her hand and squeezed it, while Adora looked on with a mixture of concern and embarrassment. Fortunately, the emotional storm passed before they had to raise their heads. Isabella dried her eyes and smiled at Cobola and Adora, albeit feebly. She neither went forward to give her life to Christ when the pastor's invitation came, nor did she express a desire to visit the church again, echoing Cobola's opinion that everybody present was much too young for her.

'But it was much better than the Cathedral-o,' she said. 'I will continue to look.'

Cobola sighed inwardly, wondering what would happen when Isabella found a church that suited her. While resting in bed that afternoon, she thought of about it again, and wondered what had caused those tears during the service. As she continued her reflection, she remembered the chorus being sung at the time and decided that it must have been its words that had affected Isabella. From that conclusion she drew another: that while putting on a brave face, Isabella was harbouring fear.

Two weeks later, Ilara called Isabella to say she had been making inquiries on her behalf and that she had heard people in her salon talking about a new ministry started by a Nigerian called Pastor Hezekiah. She offered to go to his church with Isabella if she needed company though, being a staunch Roman Catholic, she had no desire to experience another form of worship. She didn't hide her relief when Isabella thanked her for the offer but said she was sure Nanna would agree to accompany her again. Indeed, now that Cobola thought she knew why Isabella needed a more uplifting form of worship, she readily agreed to go with her to the service.

Yao tightened his lips when she mentioned it, and said sulkily,

'Nanna, why are you encouraging Bella?'

'What do you mean encouraging Bella?' Cobola retorted, 'And don't use that tone with me… Bella is a grown woman. Instead of getting angry, you should be asking her why, after putting up with the Cathedral for twenty years, all of a sudden she's so determined to find another church.'

If anything, Cobola's apparent siding with Isabella increased Yao's opposition to her desire to find a greener spiritual pasture. It was only for his mother's sake, that he agreed that on his way to the Cathedral with Adora, he would drop them off by the school in whose assembly hall Pastor Hezekiah held his services and, having done so, barely acknowledged their thanks and goodbyes before zooming away.It was with varying degrees of uneasiness that the two women made their way up a slight incline.

The assembly hall was impossible to miss. A huge white banner hung over the entrance, with HOPE OF GLORY MINISTRY, PASTOR: A.A. HEZEKIAH, emblazoned on it in blue and green. Apart from their visit to the Assemblies of God church, Cobola had also watched many charismatic services on television, so she now knew what to expect, more or less. Indeed, there was an atmosphere of excitement in the hall which was filled to capacity, mainly with women, most of whom seemed to be in their late thirties and above. Isabella's pleased expression made it clear that she already felt quite at home. Soon after they took their seats, a high-chested, middle-aged woman announced a half-an-hour session of what she called, 'Praise and Worship' and, in a voice more powerful than melodious, led the congregation in a series of rousing choruses, accompanied on a keyboard by a young man, one of the few in the congregation. The women danced and swayed in their seats as they sang, generating so much additional heat that, despite the twirling ceiling fans, Cobola had to make use of the woven, hand-held one Yao and Isabella had brought her from Accra. 'Praise and worship' wound down with a chorus she knew and liked, coming, as it did, from the first line of one of her favourite psalms. This time she joined in the singing though, slightly overcome by the heat, she did so sitting down and only swayed a little:

> *Bless the Lord O my soul,*
> *And all that is within me bless his holy name.*
> *Bless the Lord O my soul,*
> *And all that is within me bless his holy name.*
> *He has done great things,*
> *He has done great things,*
> *He has done great things,*
> *Bless His holy name.*

A five-minute hiatus followed, during which the young man performed musical acrobatics on the keyboard to maintain the congregation's excitement. Then, amid rapturous applause, Pastor Hezekiah entered the hall with his arms aloft, shouting, 'Hallelujah! in a deep, compelling voice.

His strong Yoruba accent suggested that he had spent most of his life in Nigeria but, in all other respects, he could have passed for a graduate of one of the colleges that trained the American evangelists Cobola had seen on TV: striding up and down the stage with a large open Bible in one hand and, as if his congregation cared, mentioning ancient Greek words that had been translated into English in the passage. He peppered every other statement with a 'Hallelujah' or a 'Can I have an ay-men?' and from time to time, as if struck by the Holy Spirit, suddenly paused, mid-sentence, to speak in tongues. Isabella seemed enthralled, but Cobola doubted that Pastor Hezekiah was genuinely spiritual – too sharply dressed and barbered, in her opinion, for someone who spent hours communing with the Lord; and there was also something unnatural about his complexion that suggested skin-bleaching. But, there was no denying his charisma, and she knew, with a sinking heart, that Isabella had already fallen under his spell. After a long and, as far as she was concerned, rambling sermon, he held up his hand to prevent the choir from starting another chorus, declaring,

'I have received a word of from the Lord. A sister has been drawn to this place today for a special reason. She has a torment in her soul...The Lord Jesus said, "Come unto me all you that are heavy-laden, and I will give you rest." Sister, the Lord is going to deliver you today. Right now. Come up and receive your healing...'

To Cobola's astonishment, he seemed to be staring straight at them and, in spite of her misgivings, she was impressed till she remembered noticing that the other women in the room were all conservatively attired with covered arms, high necklines, no visible make-up or earrings, and heads covered with scarves or berets, whereas she and Isabella had dressed as they did to attend ordinary services at the Cathedral. In the ensuing silence, she glanced at Isabella. She was sitting with upright alertness, her eyes on the pastor. He kept his own eyes on them till, as if under a spell, Isabella rose, moved past her, and forward to the stage.

The choir now began to sing softly:

*I surrender all,*
*I surrender all,*
*All to thee my blessed saviour*
*I surrender all.*

They repeated the chorus until Isabella had climbed on to the stage and Pastor Hezekiah had again held up his hand. Gesturing to her to kneel before him, he spoke in tongues over her for a minute or so before bellowing, 'In the mighty name of *Jesus*, I command the spirit of fear tormenting our sister to leave…Leave!' Over and over he bellowed,

'Leave!' Then he touched Isabella's forehead and she crumpled at his feet. Amid loud applause and shouts of 'Hallelujah', Pastor Hezekiah knelt and prayed silently over her before helping her to rise. The high-chested woman, who turned out to be Mrs. Hezekiah, then led Isabella out by a side door. She returned to her seat about fifteen minutes later clutching leaflets, and radiating such joy that Cobola could not help but feel happy for her; yet Yao's hostility coupled with her own suspicions about the pastor, made her afraid that trouble lurked darkly on the Ennisons' horizon – like one of those ugly warships that used to come to Freetown during the Second World War.

They walked away from the service deep in their own thoughts, but while waiting by the roadside for a taxi, Cobola said to Isabella,

'Well, my dear?'

'Nanna, all I can say is that, for the first time since my operation, I feel totally well in body, mind and spirit.'

Vacant taxis were scarce on Sundays, with the result that the two women reached home after two o'clock. By that time, Yao had worked himself up into a silent fury, in spite of the care Isabella had taken to make sure that their lunch was ready before going out, and her instructions to Adora to serve her father if they had not returned by the time he was ready to eat.

140

Silence reigned as they sat down. Cobola pointedly said grace when Yao seemed unable or unwilling to speak. She also tried to make conversation, but only Adora replied in complete sentences, and even she soon lapsed into silence. After her third attempt at prompting comments from the others, Cobola pushed back her chair and stood up.

'Mr. and Mrs. Ennison,' she said, 'I'm sorry, but if I eat any more food in this room, I will have indigestion for the rest of the day. I beg to leave. And with your permission, I'll take Adora with me.'

Picking up her plate, she signalled to Adora to follow. As they left the room, Isabella apologised with a glance, but Yao didn't even raise his head. Along the corridor, Adora dashed tears from her cheeks. Cobola was no less upset, but she was angry as well and remained dry-eyed. While they were trying to eat, Adora said,

'Nanna, why is Daddy is so angry with Mummy?'

'Darling, men don't like their lives to change, especially when they don't think it is necessary.'

'So if Mummy continues to go to that church, Daddy will be angry with her every Sunday,' Adora said.

Since Cobola could provide no assurance to the contrary, Adora went on sadly, 'Sunday used to be my best time with them.'

'Try not to worry…ya?' Cobola answered. 'They'll sort themselves out. Let's go and rest.'

Yao remained at the table while Isabella cleared away their unfinished meal and washed the dishes.

'So this is what I'll have to put up with if you start going to that church every Sunday.' He sounded angry but was, in fact, churned up with anxiety.

'Yao, I have to go back,' Isabella said as she sat down beside him. 'You don't know what that Pastor did for me today.'

'And that's another thing,' Yao answered. 'Nanna hinted that there might be something the matter with you. How come *I* wasn't aware of that? Have you forgotten what I said about shutting me out? I was talking about every part of your life, Bella, not just your body.'

'There *was* something wrong with me, but there was no point telling you about it; you wouldn't have been able to help me…And I hadn't discussed it with Nanna; she was only guessing… Yao, when Pastor Hezekiah – that's his name – touched my head today, it was as if he lifted a load from my shoulders. Only an anointed man of God could have done that.'

Yao stared at her with scornful incredulity.

142

'I would never have thought someone with a good degree would be so gullible. Anointed my foot! Most of these guys start their churches only to make money. Just you wait; in two years' time your anointed pastor will have built a church bigger than State House.'

His superior attitude so infuriated Isabella that, despite her previous desire to avoid a quarrel, she said hotly,

'What gives you the right to judge him, Yao? Even if many of them are fakes, what makes you so sure this pastor doesn't have a genuine gift for healing? How do you explain the warmth I felt all over my body when he touched me? And that I immediately felt as if a load had been lifted from my shoulders – a load I'd been carrying since two thousand and seven. And that I fell to the ground though he didn't push me?…How do you explain all that? '

Had Yao felt less threatened by Isabella's outburst in favour of the pastor, and by the likelihood that what he feared was bound to happen now, it would have struck him as significant that she mentioned two thousand and seven, which was the year she had been treated for cancer. Instead all that registered, and it upset him more, was that Isabella had kept a secret from him for three years.

'I'm not listening to any more of this nonsense,' he said, with uncharacteristic rudeness, and left the room.

Isabella put her head on the table and groaned with frustration. Pastor Hezekiah had removed one burden from her shoulders and Yao seemed determined to lay another one there. Well, I'm not going to let him, she said to herself with sudden resolve and, echoing Ilara's remark, muttered: After all, *I* was the one suffering.

Cobola listened to Adora's gentle snores, envying her the ability to relieve her anxiety with sleep. Exhausted as she was, she couldn't even close her eyes to rest them. Lord, this is too much for me-o, she muttered and, feeling the need for a flesh and blood confidante as well, phoned Gertrude to say she was coming to have breakfast with her the next day – early. She would take advantage of the Ennisons' morning run.

The atmosphere in the Volvo was as strained as it had been at lunch the previous day, so it was with a sense of relief that Cobola said, 'Have a nice day, my dears,' when Sheku pulled up outside Gertrude's house.

'It's only leftovers-o,' Gertrude warned before asking Sia to bring in their breakfast which was small pieces of boiled cassava shaped into balls, and a light soup made with palm oil and lady fish. Gertrude had introduced Cobola to this dish when they shared an apartment many years before, and it had become one of her favourites.

'Trudy don't apologise,' she said. 'You know it always tastes better the next day, and in any case, I came to talk...I'm seriously worried.'

'My sister, you are right to be,' Gertrude said when Cobola had told her what she knew of Sunday's events. 'It can cause problems-o, when one person becomes more religious than the other, or even changes religion. Did I ever tell you about Auntie Elpina? She became a follower of that prophet Adejobi; you know the one – Church of the Lord Aladurah...In the end, her husband went to live with one of his girlfriends and never came home again. Why do you think I agreed to become a Jehovah's Witness before I married Abu? I wanted peace in my home and Abu, as you know, was staunch. I don't believe everything they say-o – that thing about only one hundred and forty-four thousand people going to heaven...And, as for not accepting blood transfusions, I just thank God that none of us ever lost enough blood to need one. I don't know what I would have done in that situation...'

In almost a lifetime of friendship, this was one of the few occasions that Gertrude's conversation didn't hold Cobola's attention. Interrupting the flow, she said with resignation,

'I just have to continue to beg God to show Himself.'

'Cobs, that's all you can do… But who would have thought Yao would change like that? I remember how you used to complain about him allowing Bella to wear the trousers.'

'Either she didn't do anything he objected to in those early days, or he was so in love that she was just perfect in his eyes. Not that he doesn't love her now-o; I know he does, but they've been married twenty years, and she's doing something he definitely doesn't want her to do…'

'So, he's making her life difficult,' Gertrude said. 'Men are like that,'

'Kweku was never like that,' Cobola answered and set her lips in a firm line.

'Have you forgotten how he ignored you for three whole days? I'm telling you; men are like that. Even the good ones. Kweku taught you a lesson and you never offended him again; that's why you had such a happy and peaceful home.'

Cobola still disagreed with Gertrude but, not being in the mood for an argument, even a friendly one, she said, 'Perhaps you're right...What is really upsetting Yao is that he thinks Bella is going to become too holy for him.'

'Then tell him to go easy with her. If he continues to be difficult, and Isabella tells the pastor, instead of advising her to submit to her husband, he might tell her that Christians have to be prepared to be persecuted. I've heard that some of them do that to keep their female membership high. If Isabella listens to him, she won't compromise, not even to have peace in her home.'

Gertrude's words proved prophetic. Yao listened politely to his mother's advice but made no comment, and in the following weeks Isabella seemed to embrace the version of Christianity taught by the charismatic Pastor Hezekiah. She changed her elegant wardrobe to be like other members of the church, and having discarded trousers herself, tried to make Adora abandon her jeans, and the little shorts she wore around the house, referring to scriptures that suggested not only that women wearing men's clothing displeased God, but that braids, gold earrings and pearls were also to be avoided. With Yao's vociferous support, Adora continued to wear the clothes she liked, and they no longer waited for Isabella for Sunday lunch which Cobola now preferred to have alone. On Wednesday evenings,

Isabella rushed through her evening meal to attend a prayer meeting and Bible class at Pastor Hezekiah's house, while Yao dismissed Sheku early and joined his colleagues for drinks after work instead of coming straight home as he used to.

It was on one such Wednesday evening that Cobola heard frantic cries of 'Nanna! Nanna! Nanna!' close to her apartment. The high, desperate voice was Adora's. The tense atmosphere in the house had worsened Cobola's aches and pains, but with her heart pounding so hard she thought it might stop, she struggled up from the couch and limped to the corridor as fast as she could. There, she faced an appalling scene : Adora twisting and turning to escape Yao's raised arm while, wringing her hands, Khadi begged him to have pity on the girl.

Yao's arm came down on Adora's shoulder. She yelped with pain but still couldn't escape. Realising that only some dramatic intervention would stop her father from hitting her again, Cobola let out a deep groan, clutching at her chest.

Khadi shouted, 'Lord have mercy! Mr. Yao, look at Nanna!' She caught Cobola as she seemed about to fall and, alarmed as he was meant to be, Yao let go of Adora and rushed into the kitchen for a glass of water. As if she'd had enough sorrow for one day, Adora fled to her bedroom, sobbing.

Cobola allowed Yao to feed her some of the water before asking him to take her back to her apartment. With Khadi anxiously in tow, he helped her into her sitting-room, laid her on the couch and asked if he should call her doctor.

'That won't be necessary,' Cobola said, her firmness startling in someone so recently about to collapse. 'Khadi, you may go; thank you...ya?'

Remembering that tone of voice from two years back, Khadi dared not linger.

'There's nothing the matter with me,' Cobola said when she was alone with Yao. 'I just wanted you to stop beating my granddaughter...Yao.'

'Yes, Nanna,'

'Sit down.'

Yao did as told.

'Yao...'

Yes, Nanna.

'Why?...Have you been drinking, or what?'

'I found Adora at the gate with a boy, Nanna. He was kissing her.'

Had Yao come to report that incident, Cobola would have volunteered to give Adora a talking-to. Outraged as she was by his behaviour, she said with withering coldness,

'And for that you humiliated the poor girl in front of Khadi and didn't care where your hand

149

landed? You, her father? Shame on you!...You only beat her because you are angry with her mother. Shame on you! '

Yao muttered an apology after a moment but, as if she couldn't bear the sight of him, Cobola turned her back and closed her eyes. Another minute passed, before she heard him get up and leave. She'd only pretended to be ill, but she was truly distressed and it took a while for her to summon the strength to go to Adora's room. There, she sat on the bed holding Adora's limp hand for some time before saying, 'Darling, stop crying...ya? Come.' Whispering more comforting words, she led Adora to her own room and bed. About two hours later, Isabella knocked on her door, clearly distraught. Apparently, Khadi had gone to wait by the gate and had told her what happened in her absence.

Adora turned her back on her mother, refusing to speak and, in the end, Cobola felt she had to intervene.

'Just leave her for tonight, Bella,' she said in a low voice. 'She's very hurt.' Whereupon, Isabella said, 'Thank you, Nanna. Goodnight,' and stalked out.

Feeling less sympathetic towards Adora now, Cobola sent her to sleep in Ida's room. She was pouring hot water from her flask to soothe herself with a cup of Milo when she became aware of furious voices on the other side of the house. She pressed her ear against the connecting door – just in time to hear Isabella shout,

'I will say it again, Yao – whether you like it or not. You are just dancing around Christianity.'

To which Yao responded with equal passion, 'If neglecting your husband and family is what true Christianity is about, I will continue to dance around it…There was peace and love in this home before that pastor took over your life. He might as well be your boyfriend.'

'Ay, Yao,' Cobola muttered, covering her ears in case he said something worse. More distressed than ever, she retreated to her bedroom and, for a whole hour, sat up in bed having what she called 'a session' with God. It had been years since she asked God for favours, preferring to express only gratitude for blessings in her prayers; but that night she pleaded for Yao and Isabella to be saved from destroying their marriage, their home, and themselves.

The situation seemed no better in the morning. Yao came to inquire after her health and offer another apology, but left for work without Isabella who tried again to see Adora before going to look for a taxi. Adora refused to open the door, even when her grandmother ordered her to.

Cobola was playing with her chubby, cheerful namesake to comfort herself, when she heard Adora say,

'Good morning, Nanna.'

She didn't even glance Adora's way, let alone return the greeting. Adora hovered. Cobola called out to Ida to relieve her of the child then, in her iciest tone, told Adora to stand before her.

'You disrespected your mother last night and the two of us this morning. Why?'

'Nanna, I'm sorry, but it's Mummy who has caused all this trouble,' Adora answered, her bottom lip pushed out in a pout.

'Miss lady, that is *not* for you to judge,' Cobola said in the same frigid voice. 'Not only is she your mother, she's three times your age...You will apologise to her this evening, your hear me? Otherwise, I will lock my door on you.'

Fresh tears welled under Adora's swollen eyelids, but after another sulky minute she promised to do as told. Cobola then patted the space beside her.

'Come and sit down...Daddy told me why he beat you.'

'Nanna, we were not doing anything bad,' Adora said, her voice rising with renewed indignation and impending tears. 'Chimah met me waiting for a *poda-poda* at PZ and came home with me as far as the gate. He only kissed my cheek to say goodbye, but Daddy saw him and started shouting at us…He got out of the car and chased Chimah away, and then… and then, he opened the back door and pushed me inside.'

'I'm very sorry to hear that,' Cobola said, 'but fathers are always worried when they catch boys kissing their daughters, and your father is already upset – you know that…In fact, I'm going to ask you to do something you'll find even harder than apologising to your mother…When you come home this evening, go and tell Daddy you are sorry about yesterday – forget that you didn't deserve the way he behaved. Just say you are sorry. Will you do that for me?'

'Yes, Nanna.'

'And give him a hug for me…ya?'

Adora sagged against her but, though sniffing away tears, again promised to do as she asked.

'Alright… let's talk about something else.' Cobola said briskly, 'So you still like this Chimah boy.'

As she had hoped, there was a smile in Adora's voice when she answered.

'Yes, Nanna; but he's just a friend.'

'Good. Let him remain so for now, you hear? I was only a little bit older than you when Uncle

Orlando was born. It would kill me if that happened to you.'

When a previously unknown uncle entered their lives, Yao's explanation to his children had been that their grandmother had had two husbands, and that Orlando had grown up in America. Aged seven at the time, Adora, had little curiosity about people outside her immediate family and had had no desire to know more than she'd been told. Realising now that her father had left out significant details, she was longing to ask questions; but she sensed that that was not a story her grandmother wished to share, and merely continued to gaze at her.

'You can bring Chimah to visit me one Saturday after your lesson,' Cobola went on. 'Would you like that?'

'Yes, Nanna, but he might not want to come; not after what happened. I'll ask him.'

'Alright. And *I* will talk to Daddy and Mummy about it when things calm down.'

'Do you think they'll be friends again?'

As much to reassure herself as Adora, Cobola answered, 'I know it doesn't seem like that now, but they will. When husbands and wives quarrel, that doesn't mean they don't love each other anymore.'

'Enh,' Adora said. Her doubtful expression and tone made Cobola say, with a smile,

'You'll see.'

154

Adora apologised to her mother as she had promised to do and was still cuddling with her remorseful father when an anguished cry tore them apart. It came from the kitchen where Isabella had been having a word with Khadi. Father and daughter rushed to see what had happened, colliding with Khadi who had charged out of the kitchen to fetch Yao. Looking the picture of devastation, Isabella was on the kitchen floor. Yao crouched beside her, concern creasing his forehead.

'Bella, what is it?' he asked, 'What has happened?'

'Papa has been shot.'

Yao sank back on his haunches, too shocked for words and, though she barely remembered her grandfather, Adora covered her mouth with both hands as her eyes flew open. Isabella went on in a lifeless voice,

'Lily says he's dying.'

Her mobile phone had fallen out of her hand and lay beside her. Still stunned, Yao picked it up and clicked on the most recent caller. As he expected, it was Isabella's sister, Lillian. She told him, between sobs, that their father had been coming home from his barber on a Washington D.C. street, when he was caught in the crossfire of a gun battle over drugs between two gangs of black youth. A stray bullet had torn through his gut. He had had emergency surgery, but wasn't expected to survive the night.

'Oh, Lily! I'm sorry,' Yao said. Tears pricked his eyes because he was fond of his father-in-law. 'Hush, ya?...*I* won't be able to come, but Bella will be there as soon as we can arrange it. How is Mama T. bearing up?'

'She's not,' Lillian said. 'I'm afraid for her too. The shock was too much.'

'Then we won't talk to her tonight; just tell her we send love, okay?...Hush, ya? Be strong.'

Meanwhile, Khadi had rushed to tell Cobola the tragic news, guessing correctly that her restrictions didn't apply in an emergency. Arriving on the scene soon afterwards, Cobola found Adora saying comforting words to Isabella who was sobbing in Yao's arms. Shocked and saddened though she was, Cobola still sent up a prayer of thanksgiving. The tragedy had obviously suspended, if not ended, the Ennisons' hostilities and would separate Isabella from her Pastor Hezekiah for a while – all to the good, as far as Cobola was concerned. She had no idea how the situation would finally be resolved, but neither did she have any doubt that events were somehow moving in that direction. She was, therefore, not in the least surprised when Orlando called her a couple of days later.

Sounding unusually cool, he said, 'Nanna, I'm a little hurt. Every time I've called these past weeks, all of you have sounded strange, yet you've kept assuring me that all is well. I know all isn't well, so please put me in the picture before Bella comes over. After all, I'm family. If Yao didn't have this tragedy on his hands, I would have tackled him about it...'

Immediately contrite, Cobola said. 'My dear, please forgive me. I had wanted to tell you about it, but I didn't like talking behind their backs...Yao and Isabella have quarrelled...'

'Uh-oh.'

'Yes. Bella started going to a charismatic church and...'

'Say no more. I went down that road with Beverly twenty years ago...'

'*Enh*!'

'Yes. We were going through a really rough patch in our marriage – all my fault.'

'If you ask me, they are both at fault; and now the whole thing has got out of hand.'

'That bad, eh?'

'That bad, though the atmosphere has been better since this terrible news from Washington. Yao even behaved himself when Isabella's Pastor Hezekiah and wife came to offer their condolences and pray for the family. Fortunately the pastor didn't speak in tongues that day…'

'Yes,' Orlando said with amusement, 'I don't imagine that would have gone down well with Yao.'

'You've said it…So, tell me. How did you solve your own problem?'

'Well, Beverly forgave me after a while. She dragged me to her new church, but I only went there for a short time. Couldn't take all that rowdiness and showmanship.'

'A diehard Episcopalian,' Cobola said with a chuckle. 'I, too, find those services draining.'

'But one good thing,' Orlando went on, 'it made me more interested in reading the Bible. Bev and I began reading it together, which led quite naturally to praying together. That's what brought us close again. In the end she decided to come back to our church…'

'I don't see Yao ever agreeing to go to Pastor Hezekiah's church – even if they make it up…'

'Another diehard, eh?' Orlando said.

'Not only that. He dislikes this whole born-again business, and, to be honest, I think he has a point where Bella is concerned. She has become… You'll see for yourself if you manage to get together while she's over there.'

'Yao says she's coming over for two weeks, and I'll make sure she spends a couple of days with us. Perhaps we'll be able to help...'

'Whatever you do, please don't let her know I told you anything.'

'We'll handle it carefully, Nanna. Don't worry. Meanwhile, *you* work on Yao.'

'I'll do my best, my dear. Perhaps he'll be more willing to listen to me when Bella is not around.'

'I sure hope so. This year of all years, you shouldn't have a situation like this on your hands. We have to celebrate that eightieth birthday.'

'You know something? With one thing and another I'd completely forgotten about that.'

'Well *we* haven't, and we're coming...'

'God bless you, my dear. And give my love to Beverly.'

'She sent you hers.'

That conversation comforted Cobola enough to make her feel like switching on her television and browsing through the channels for a good Nigerian movie; but she resisted the urge, feeling it would be wrong to be enjoying herself while, just down the corridor, Isabella was deep in sorrow.

# TWELVE

*Health for the World*, where Isabella worked, was an American non-governmental agency. Consequently, an endorsement on its official letterhead, and a scanned invitation from her sister were all it took for her to obtain the necessary visas in record time. In bed, on the night before her departure, she said,

'Yao, are you awake?'

'Mhm.'

'Can I say something?'

'Mhm.'

Not the response she had hoped for, but she went on to thank Yao for the help he'd given her with her travel arrangements, saying she hadn't taken it for granted. 'And Yao, I beg. Please forgive me for not telling you I had a problem. I honestly thought it was better that way.'

'Babes, do you realise I still don't know exactly what it was?' Yao answered. 'Anyway, we'll talk about that when you come back...This is not the time.'

'Okay,' Isabella said – in small voice, because though Yao had been kind since her father's death, he didn't seem to have forgiven her; but she took comfort from the fact that he'd called her 'Babes' – something he hadn't done for a long time.

'My dear, come and sit beside me,' Cobola said when Ida let Isabella into her apartment the next morning. The night before, she'd sent Adora with a message to say she hoped Isabella could spare her fifteen minutes before leaving for the airport. Bereaved or not, the old Isabella would never have appeared in public with her head wrapped tightly in a scarf, a long sleeved blouse, buttoned up to her neck, and no earrings; but, despite the depressing drabness of her attire, Cobola was delighted that she'd come early enough for them to talk.

'I know you are not going to America for enjoyment, my dear, but I hope I'll see more flesh on you when you come back. You are *too* thin.'

Isabella answered with a feeble smile, 'Nanna, I'll try.'

'Good...First of all, let me give you this sympathy card. I've addressed it to your mother, but it's for the whole family. I'm sending two hundred dollars as my own small contribution to the funeral expenses.'

'God bless you, Nanna.'

'Now, the other thing I wanted to see you about...I believe people who love each other should be able to sort out their differences without a third

161

party interfering, but it seems you and Yao haven't been able to do that, so I want you to hear what *I* think about what has been going on. Don't say anything; just listen…ya? I'm not a pastor-o,' she went on. 'I don't know theology, but God has given me intelligence, I understand English well, and I read my Bible… As I told the twins, Jesus is my person. One of the reasons I love him is that he tried to make spiritual matters simple for ordinary people to understand – people like me. The first thing I want to say is that *I* have no doubt that if Jesus were to come down to earth today he would condemn all these rules about how people should dress and not dress, and what they shouldn't eat or drink that some churches use to control their members. He was always more concerned about people's hearts and minds, and about their actions, than about how they seemed on the outside. The other thing I want to say is that when some Pharisees tried to trap him over whether or not it was right for Jews to pay taxes, he told them to give Caesar the things that were Caesar's and God the things that were God's. Remember?'

Isabella nodded and Cobola said, 'Well, my dear, the way I see your situation, Yao is your Caesar. Unless you can bring him round to your new way of thinking, you will have to find a way to balance your church activities with keeping him happy; otherwise your marriage will no longer be nice…Look what's happened already…Don't think I'm taking Yao's side-o. I am not. In fact, I have something to say to him as well. I agree with you that he's just been dancing around Christianity…'

Isabella gasped behind her hands which had covered her mouth. 'Nanna, you heard us?'

Cobola's lips twitched with wry humour,

'You should have remembered to close your door before you started shouting at each other.'

'I'm sorry,' Isabella murmured.

'You don't have to apologise, my dear; you were in your own house. Anyway, what you said to Yao is just what *I* told him a while back, only I didn't put it in such an interesting way...' Seeing that Isabella was still upset, Cobola said with some irritation, 'Bella, forget it. Just promise me you'll think about what I said.'

The promise given, Cobola said, 'Now, help me up; let me hug you.'

She held Isabella close, saying, 'Hush, ya. God go with you. And give my love and sympathy to your mother, Lily, and the others.'

Yao drove Isabella to the airport and stayed till it was time for her to go through departure formalities. They had little to say to each other on the ferry and while they waited for the announcement, but when the moment of parting came, strained as their relationship had been of late, Yao's eyes burned with unshed tears. When they stood to say goodbye, he held Isabella's shoulders as naturally as if they'd never quarrelled, and kissed her lightly on the lips.

'Call me as soon as you get there-o,' he murmured.

Isabella had her handbag in one hand and her carry-on luggage in the other. Incapable of speech, she merely nodded, expressing her own emotions with welling eyes. A porter stood waiting for her beside the trolley carrying her luggage. She followed him to the entrance of Departures without a backward glance, and soon vanished from Yao's sight.

There was no return ferry until nine-thirty which meant that, in spite of relatively free flowing traffic, it was well after eleven o'clock when Yao reached Murray Town and home. He unlatched the gate and drove slowly into the compound, unaware that two masked men had been lurking in nearby bushes. Bent almost double, they followed him inside and remained hidden beside the car until he came out to padlock the gate for the night. That was when one of the men startled him with a jostle and poked the sharp point of a knife through his shirt. Trying not to show alarm, Yao muttered a curse.

'Mr. Ennison,' the man said as he fished for Yao's mobile phone and wallet with his free hand. 'If you know what is good for you, don't talk. Just go inside the house.'

Area boys, Yao guessed, since they knew his name. For some reason, that calmed his pounding heart and steadied his hands as he put his key in the lock of the metal gate protecting the front door, and then opened the door itself. He couldn't hear the generator, but there was a light on in the corridor which meant that the national grid had supplied the power that night. He hoped the robbers would take what they wanted and leave without waking Khadi, whose room was at the back of the house, or Adora and his mother who slept on the other side.

The man, who had spoken, was obviously the leader. It was he who ordered Yao to leave the front door open and take them to his bedroom.

Cursing under his breath, Yao obeyed.

'Where is your wife?' demanded the other man who held an open flick knife. The answer didn't come fast enough, and he slapped Yao's face with a palm as hard as board. Yao winced, and his eyes stung; but he didn't give them the satisfaction of hearing him cry out.

'She has travelled.'

'Enh. But you know where she keeps her gold jewelleries,' the leader said. .

'The only gold jewellery my wife has is her wedding ring and she 's gone with it,' Yao told them. 'She has silver. You want that?'

'Let us see.'

Yao opened Isabella's bedside drawer and showed them her small collection of silver chains and earrings, and the inexpensive bead creations she also liked. He cringed as their filthy fingers pawed over the various items before stuffing their pockets with those they thought they could sell. The leader then grabbed Yao's wrist, inspected his watch, decided it was worth something, and told him to remove it.

'Okay. Now give us the rest of your money.'

'What 'rest,'? Yao said through clenched teeth. 'All the money I have is with you – in my wallet.'

The robber flipped the wallet open and withdrew its contents.

'But this is nothing,' he said with a look of contempt.

166

'Well, it's all I have,' Yao answered. 'Even if you stab all my body, and turn the house upside down, you won't find anything. We don't keep money here…' Such was his revulsion that, though he knew he was risking injury, he couldn't stop himself from adding, 'because of bastards like you,'

'Mr. Ennison, if you say something like that again, you will regret it-o,' the leader said. 'I have told you not to talk.'

'Let us go and find his mother,' his partner suggested. 'She lives here. These old Krio women always have gold.'

'You are right…I have seen them going to weddings with thick bracelets and chains.'

Yao's fear, which had receded when he realised the robbers were area boys, came rushing back at the thought of such criminals approaching his mother and daughter.

'I beg you,' he said, 'leave the poor woman in peace. She's old.'

The leader answered amiably enough, 'If she gives us what we want, we won't hurt her.' But his attitude hardened again when Yao made no immediate move. He said,

'Mr. Ennison, don't waste our time-o…'

'Then lend me my phone, let me call her,' Yao said. 'I don't want you to bang on the door.'

That request granted, he clicked on Cobola's number. Her drowsy voice answered after three rings. He said with deliberate gentleness,

'Nanna, it's me…Yao. I'm back from the airport, but there are some unfriendly visitors in the house…You understand me, eh?'

Cobola's heart jumped and raced, but taking her cue from Yao, she answered quietly, 'Yes, my dear, I understand.'

'Okay. We are coming to your place now, so please open the door. They only want money, your gold jewellery and your mobile.'

Yao didn't hear her say, 'Yes, my dear, ' because the robber had snatched the phone from him.

Determined to remain as calm as possible, Cobola took her time. Consequently, Yao and the robbers were outside the connecting door before she had reached it herself. Yao pleaded with the robbers to give her a minute or two, and when he thought she must be close, tapped on the panel.

'Nanna, we are here,' he said, keeping his voice low so as not to waken Adora. As he'd hoped, Cobola let them in almost at once, but before they could all move into her bedroom Adora's door knob turned.

'Darling, go back to bed. Go back to bed,' Cobola called out quickly. But it was too late. Adora appeared at her doorway and let out a shriek at the sight of her father with a knife to his back and two scary masked men.

'Sweetheart, don't be afraid,' Yao said, but his knees suddenly weakened, and he felt a trembling inside. It grew worse when the leader nudged him and said with a leer,

'Mr. Ennison, your daughter is fine-o.'

'If you touch her, I'll kill you with my bare hands,' Yao growled.

The leader gave a scornful chuckle.

'Mr. Ennison. You think we will just stand here with our arms folded waiting for you to kill us, eh? Anyway, women are not what sends us to heaven... Baby, go back to your room.'

'I beg. Let her stay,' Cobola said.

'Alright, but hurry up. We want to go.'

Over the years, Cobola had perfected the art of hiding valuables in places servants wouldn't think of looking, such as underneath the wool and canvas in her embroidery basket, in the deep pockets of old dresses, or in her toilet bag, but she always had some cash easily available in a drawer for market and the like. She handed about sixty thousand leones to the robbers with her mobile phone, the gold chain Kweku had given her on her fortieth birthday, and a gold bracelet she had inherited from Auntie Aina.

Intended for Adora, she'd kept the jewellery wrapped in cotton wool and stuffed in the toes of a shabby pair of shoes. Being forced to part with them was painful, but not heartbreaking. In fact, they were the first items she'd taken out.

'This is what I have,' she said.

'No, Gramma,' the leader answered with deceptive mildness. 'You have forgotten those nice gold rings on your finger.'

Cobola cried out in shock and clasped her hands together as if that would protect her wedding ring and the one with a half circle of tiny gold balls that Kweku had given her on their tenth wedding anniversary. From the floor where they had forced him to sit, Yao said, 'Don't you people have any mercy?'

'Mr. Ennison, what did I tell you?' the leader answered. 'If you talk once more; just once more...' Leaving the threat hanging in the air, he went on, ' Yes, Gramma, we want the rings.'

Yao bowed his head and held it in both hands while Adora looked on fearfully, tears flooding her cheeks. After that single cry, however, as if she were talking to someone else, Cobola said, 'Never mind, you are no longer married, and they were going to go to the grave with you.' She began to remove the rings only to discover that they wouldn't move past the middle knuckle of her finger. Having heard horrific stories of armed robbers pulling off women's wedding rings with their teeth, at first she panicked; then she sent up a prayer and, mustering all her courage, said, 'Just give me two minutes; let me go to the bathroom.'

The second robber followed her and watched impassively as, praying all the time, she slathered the rings and her finger with soap, and tugged, and tugged. 'Thank God!' she breathed when, after several attempts, they eased past her knuckle and off her finger. To avoid skin contact with the robber, she dropped them into his palm, saying with the utmost disdain,

'Here; I leave you to God.'

He didn't answer; just handed them over to his partner who was guarding Yao. Without further ado, they left the room and, apparently, the house because a strange silence descended.

Cobola fell back against her pillows.

'Nanna, hush ya,' Adora crooned. She was about to climb on the bed and cuddle up to her grandmother when, noticing that Yao was still on the floor with his head in his hands, Cobola told her in a low voice to go and help him up.

'No, I'm alright,' Yao said. 'I just need a minute.'

Indeed, a short time afterwards, he took Cobola's hand and kissed her ring finger.

'Nanna, I'm so sorry. You okay?'

'Yes, my dear, I'm okay,' Cobola answered, 'but a bit of brandy would be nice. You have some?'

'Yes... Adora, look in the sitting-room cabinet and bring the bottle with two glasses while I go and lock up...ya? Everything is open – the front door, the gate, the car...I just hope they haven't stolen from it.'

'Daddy, I want to come with you,' Adora said at once.

'Alright, sweetheart, you can be my lookout; but go get the brandy first so I can pour some for Nanna.'

While they waited for Adora, Cobola asked how the robbers had entered their compound, but Yao said,

'Nanna, let me go and come.'

He looked so exhausted that in their absence Cobola decided that it would be best for them all to get to bed as soon as possible.

'I hope you are not working tomorrow...' she said as Yao gulped his own brandy.

'No, but I'll have to go out in the morning as usual. Apart from seeing my boss to tell him I need a day off, I have to get hold of another mobile before

Bella tries to call me. Fortunately, there's a four-hour time difference…'

'Don't tell Bella anything-o,' Cobola warned. 'Let's not upset her more,'

'Don't worry, Nanna, I won't,'

'Alright, come for a hug,' she said. 'Adora, you too.'

They held each other tightly for a minute or so before Yao released himself and kissed them goodnight. Adora spent the rest of the night with her grandmother, which was an added comfort for them both. Yao had no such consolation. Lying flat on his back after a quick shower, he stared at the ceiling, reliving the experience. What is happening? he asked himself: first, trouble with Bella, then her father is shot, then armed robbers... He said aloud, 'If I'd been brought up differently, tomorrow I would go and consult an *alfa.*' That was his last thought. Helped by the swig of brandy, he soon drifted off to sleep.

His final thought of the night was exactly the advice Khadi gave him the next morning, after crying out and shedding tears over what had occurred while she was blissfully asleep. Since Cobola wasn't with them, she didn't hesitate to offer it while Yao was having a cup of coffee in the kitchen.

'Mr. Yao, it's just that you people say you don't believe these things. I know a good *alfa*. He will tell you why all this is happening and what you should do…'

'But Khadi, are you not a Christian?' Yao asked, pretending to be shocked.

'Yes, Mr. Yao, I'm a Christian,' Khadi answered, unabashed. 'I go to church and I pray to God, but when I have problems I feel better when I go to the *alfa*. God is *far*.'

'Don't let Nanna hear you saying that-o.'

'*No-o*!' Khadi agreed, widening her eyes and covering her mouth in mock dismay. 'But you should call a pastor to come and pray.'

'I'll leave that to Nanna,' Yao said. 'By the way, if Miss Bella calls you from America, don't say one word about the armed robbers, you hear me?...I know you and your big mouth…'

Khadi lowered her eyes, remembering how incensed Yao had been when he realised that it was she who had told Isabella that he hit Adora.

'I won't tell her anything, Mr. Yao.'

'Good.'

Ida and Sheku arrived soon afterwards, and having no objection to Khadi telling them about the robbery, Yao went to collect his car keys.

As he and Sheku approached the Congo Cross Police Station en route to the city centre, he wondered aloud if it was worth reporting the robbery.

'I can't even describe the bastards,' he said. 'They hid their faces.'

Sheku had become slightly more communicative towards him since marrying Ida. He said, 'If they are area boys, the police will know them, Mr. Yao.'

'You are right, and even if I don't get my own things back, perhaps they'll arrest them before they go and distress other people...Okay stop.'

Having submitted his statement to the police, Yao proceeded into town to carry out his errands. He returned home soon after midday, went straight to bed and was so deep in sleep when Isabella called, that he couldn't suppress yawns while she was bringing him up to date. In the end, she asked, puzzled,

'Yao, why are you so tired in the middle of the day?'

'I didn't get enough sleep last night. The ferry was delayed.'

'Ooh. Poor you. Go to bed early.'

'I intend to,' Yao said. 'My love to all, and take care, ya?'

'Same message to Nanna and Adora...'

Isabella wanted to send an additional message to Adora, but Yao yawned again and, realising that she didn't have his full attention, she said, 'Never mind; tomorrow.'

'Alright, Babes. Bye.'

Isabella was frowning when she clicked off. It was unlike her normally resilient husband to be exhausted merely because he'd gone to bed a few hours later than usual. The mystery deepened when she called Khadi to remind her to change his bath towel and make sure he had enough clean boxer shorts before going away for the weekend.

'How did Mr. Yao seem this morning?' she asked. 'He sounded very tired when I talked to him just now.'

'It must be that you woke him up, Miss Bella.'

'What do you mean, I woke him up? Didn't he go to work today?'

'He went, ma, but he came home early. I don't know why.'

Isabella then tried calling Cobola. Her puzzlement increased when an electronic voice told her that the phone was currently switched off. That had never happened before. Her mind was on her father's funeral, however, and Yao seemed perfectly all right the next time they spoke to each other. She didn't pursue the matter.

Cobola woke up with an aching, swollen knuckle on her left hand, and sharp pains in her ankle and shoulders, so she decided to spend the day in bed with her Bible. As soon as she'd had her breakfast, she sent Ida round to Gertrude with a note informing her of their misfortune, but asking her not to think of visiting till the next day. 'Trudy, I am just too broken,' she wrote. Her reason for deciding to spend the day with her Bible was that after Adora had fallen asleep she, too, had lain awake for a while, mulling over the tribulations that had befallen the Ennisons in the last few months. Unlike Yao, she came to a tentative conclusion as to their cause and intended to meditate prayerfully on relevant biblical passages. In the last few years, she had started underlining those that seemed to leap out at her from the pages and by this time there were quite a number of them to go through. Concentrating on spiritual things didn't prevent her from splaying the fingers on her left hand from time to time, and feeling the prickle of tears when she looked at the paler skin where her rings had been, but by late afternoon, she had bathed, dressed, had her feet massaged, and was on the couch in her sitting-room, ready for conversation.

'Ida,' she said, 'Please go and see if Mr. Yao is awake. If he is, tell him I want to see him, then you can go home.'

'Yes, Nanna.'

Ten minutes later, Yao was beside her on the couch and she was saying, 'You are looking much better, my dear. Did you rest well?'

'Yes, Nanna. I slept like a baby. I could hardly keep my eyes open when Bella called…'

'Ah. Thank God she arrived safely.'

'Yes. The funeral is on Saturday…Here. I got you a new phone. I regret not asking those scoundrels to leave me my SIM card, but my number is there, with Bella's, Khadi's, Sheku's, and the boys'. Those are the ones I remember. Adora will help you with the rest.'

'Thank you, my dear…Now tell me, what happened last night?'

'They hid behind the car and followed me in when I opened the gate,' Yao said, and recounted the episode up to the point where the robbers forced him to bring them to her apartment.

'They knew my name, and that you live here, so they must be local thieves – maybe drug addicts, since they only wanted things they could sell quickly. I reported the theft at Congo Cross Police Station this morning, and they told me that criminal elements have recently moved to the area. They're trying to round them up but haven't found all their hideouts yet... Nanna, I feel so bad about your jewellery, especially the rings. I know what they meant to you. That was the worst part, not being able to stop them...'

'My dear, *I* am just grateful they didn't wound you. '

'Yes, it could have been worse. But, you know, before I fell asleep, I couldn't help thinking about all that has happened recently and wondering if there is a reason for it.' He added with a chuckle, 'Khadi says we should go to an *alfa*.'

Cobola sucked her teeth.

'She wouldn't dare say such a thing in front of me.'

'I told her,' Yao said, chuckling again. 'And she agreed.'

' I, too, lay awake for a long time thinking about whether all this trouble means something,' Cobola said, 'And I found an explanation...'

'You did?'

'Yes. I don't know if I'm correct-o, but I've been praying about it.'

'So, what is it?'

'That of late there has been too much anxiety in this house. Maybe when we give in to fear it blocks God's grace – like a cloud in front of the sun. He's still there-o, but his grace doesn't reach us as well as when our faith is strong. Anything can happen then.'

'Nanna, that is too deep for me.'

'Because you only dance around Christianity,' Cobola said.

Yao stared at her with his mouth open.

'Nanna, don't tell me you heard us that night.'

'Yes, I heard some of it – enough to know that the two of you are heading for big trouble if you don't sort yourselves out soon…But to come back to what I was saying, take me, for instance. I tell everybody that God is good, yet I keep on worrying about Adora coming home from school after dark…'

'You do?'

'Yes. And then *you* have been so afraid that Bella will become born-again and your nice life with her will end, and Bella was…'

'That was her problem, Nanna – she was afraid? Why didn't you tell me?'

'Not my place, my dear. I remember you saying that *I* wasn't the one who promised Bella for better for worse. Also, I was sure the reason she didn't tell you was that she didn't want to worry you; she didn't want to worry any of us.'

'So how come *you* knew?'

'I only guessed. When we went to that first church, she cried when they sang a chorus about Jesus's resurrection freeing us from fear.'

180

'And you know what she was afraid of?'

'I'm sure it was about the cancer coming back. What else? That should have occurred to you, you know.'

'It would have occurred to me had I known she was afraid, Nanna…After the first few months, she always seemed so positive. So…so *normal.*' He sounded angry at first, then remorse took over. 'You were right. I should at least have asked her whether something other than her dislike of the Anglican service was what was driving her away from the Cathedral…I was only thinking about myself, and my own happiness…'

'Yes, you were; but I'm sure she has forgiven you,' Cobola said. 'The only thing is, you have to change your attitude…'

As if he hadn't heard her, Yao continued to brood aloud, 'I accused her of not being one hundred percent committed to me when *I* was the one not being one hundred percent committed to her…'

Cobola watched with compassion as he contemplated his error. He seemed close to tears when he said, 'Nanna, I messed up…I messed up big time…'

'Yes, my dear,' she said, 'you messed up; but nobody goes through this life without messing up sometimes-o. Come. Let's go and pray before Adora comes home.'

181

She led him to her bedroom and they sat together at the small table where she sometimes had her first cup of tea.

'Hold my hands,' she said, and prayed,

'Our father and our God, first of all we thank you from the bottom of our hearts for saving us from bodily harm at the hands of those evildoers. And we thank you for taking Bella safely to America. We know you'll be with her and her family as they prepare to lay George to rest, and that you'll keep her safe and well till she comes back to us... Father, I beg you to forgive us for not trusting enough in your goodness and mercy, so that fear controlled our thoughts, and our actions instead of faith. Help us to keep our minds on you all the time, in Jesus name we pray. Amen.'

'Amen,' Yao murmured. He flicked away tears with his fingertips, and Cobola said,

'Adora will be upset if she sees those red eyes-o. Go and splash your face, then we can talk some more.'

'You know,' she went on when he rejoined her in the sitting-room, 'I 'have been thinking, and I hope you'll agree. I want us to pray together like this every evening till Bella comes back – you, Adora and me. I'm not sure about Khadi because we might want to pray about private things sometimes. Anyway, when

Bella comes back you both can decide if you want to continue and how you want to do it.'

In his state of remorseful apprehension, Yao readily agreed to her proposal. So, every night, after Adora had had her evening meal, they met in Cobola's sitting-room. With a view to encouraging Yao to embrace Christianity more closely, at least as *she* understood it, Cobola chose the passages and psalms that meant the most to her, and made either him or Adora read them out. After a week of this, Yao delighted her one night by offering to say the prayer, and then doing so with simple eloquence that suggested he was fast becoming used to talking to God.

'Trudy, I beg you; help me to pray,' she urged Gertrude when she visited her the next day.

'Why, what has happened?'

'Yao. I told you we now have evening prayers. Well, last night he offered to pray. And not only that; he did it all so naturally...I think he's been praying by himself as I advised him to.'

'*Enh*! Perhaps when Bella comes back, he'll be able to persuade her that you can be a good Christian without shouting 'Hallelujah,' and 'Ay-men' every five minutes.'

'Trudy!' Cobola chuckled, but she said, 'That's what I want you to help me pray about. That Bella will feel so uplifted at home she won't feel the need to go to that church.'

'Ay-men!' Gertrude said, and promised to start her own intercessions that very night. 'Meanwhile,' she went on, 'Let's eat. Sia got some fresh minnows yesterday evening. She has seasoned and fried them nicely…'

'Maalox, here I come,' Cobola said as she took her first handful of the delicious but indigestible snack. After she and Gertrude had been steadily munching for a while, she asked, 'Have you thought about Judith's invitation to visit her in England?'

'I want to see my grandchildren-o, but I don't think I'll go,' Gertrude answered. 'I can't be bothered with all that to-ing and fro-ing for a visa when I'm not even be sure they will give it to me…And, Cobs, what is there for me to do in England when everyone is out except watch television? These days I don't have the legs to go from place to place. Here, I have you and other people to talk to…'

'Like Festus Bangura, eh?' Cobola teased, for Abu's friend had become a regular visitor.

'Yes-o, Festus,' Gertrude answered with a chuckle. 'The young girlfriend he had has left him for a younger man. This old body can't oblige him in that department, but at least I can give him food. He says he has got used to krio food on Saturdays, so I make *fufu* and an *egusi soup* for him.'

'That's nice of you,' Cobola said. 'He deserves a reward after all his help the day Abu died.'

'Yes. And he makes me laugh…By the way, good news. Eddie has got his green card. He's coming home for Christmas.'

'*Enh*! I'm happy for him-o. And for you, Trudy. Why don't you ask Judith to come with the children for a week or two, then you can enjoy them all?'

Gertrude told her she'd been thinking about that and their conversation continued along cheerful lines till Cobola decided it was time for her afternoon nap which had become a regular feature of her day since Adora started attending the afternoon shift. She now went to bed for a full hour instead of dozing on the couch.

'Whose turn is it to phone tomorrow?' Gertrude asked as they parted.

'Mine,' Cobola said. 'I must remember to ask Yao to send me units, and to charge my phone tonight.'

# THIRTEEN

George Tucker's funeral took place two days after Isabella arrived in Washington D.C. Her arrangement with the Wests was that she would spend that first weekend and the following week quietly with her mother and sister, then fly to Atlanta on the next Friday, spend her second weekend with them and return to Washington on Sunday by a lateish flight. That would give her three more days with her family before starting on her homeward journey. In the circumstances, she would have preferred to spend all her time in Washington, but since Orlando had offered to buy her return ticket to Atlanta, and was taking the time and trouble to come to her father's funeral, she thought, and Yao concurred, that it would be ungracious to refuse.

The Wests met her at the domestic terminal of Atlanta's Hartsfield-Jackson Airport. Despite Orlando's prior warning that Isabella wasn't looking good, Beverly couldn't help blurting out,

'Girl, what you been doing to yourself? I'm sure you've lost ten pounds since the last time I saw you.'

'Beverly, it's stress,' Isabella answered, her eyes filling. 'And not only because of what happened to my dad...Things are not good between Yao and me right now.'

'Really! Honey, I just *can't* imagine that,' Beverly said. 'You both always seemed so tight...'

'We were...I'll tell you both about it; maybe tomorrow.'

Agreeing that the next day would be a better time for what promised to be a heavy conversation, Orlando said,

'We're taking you to dinner before we go home.'

'To a nice place called *Chops Lobster Bar*,' Beverly cut in. 'Hope you like seafood.'

'I love it,' Isabella said, 'Especially lobster. I don't know when last I ate lobster; it's so expensive at home ...'

'Well, you're in for a treat, honey. After that, I suggest an early night. Michael and Suzanne say they're coming over to meet you sometime tomorrow, and Ronald and Wendy have invited us for lunch Sunday...

'That's *nice*. Nanna will be pleased to know I met all the family.'

'Wendy is like you,' Beverly went on, 'she loves to cook. Come to think of it, will you write down the recipes for Jollof Rice and Groundnut Stew? I know she'd like to try them.'

'With pleasure,' Isabella answered.

'And how is Nanna?' Orlando asked.

'Fine, apart from her usual aches and pains; but she's not at all happy with Yao and me right now…'

As her voice faded, Beverly was quick to say, 'We agreed to put off talking about upsetting things till tomorrow…'

'Yes, we did,' Orlando said, and went on, 'So… Bella, if I remember rightly, this isn't your first time in the States...'

'No, the second. Remember I was away for part of the time when you came to set up the clinic? *Health for the World* had a convention for senior staff from all over the world that year. We met in New York.'

'Oh, yes. So you've not been as blown away by our excesses as Nanna was,' Orlando laughed.

'Not this time, though your country is truly amazing…That was the last time I saw my dad alive,' she added with a mournful sigh,.'

Quick off the mark again, Beverly asked how the twins were doing at medical school.

'Very well, and they're enjoying it too, though to hear them talk you'd think we sent them to some sort of concentration camp.'

'And our up and coming Whitney Houston?' Orlando asked.

'A little madam; but she, too, is doing well at school – *and* with her singing. She's going to take part in Ballanta's annual concert this year.'

Talking about her children lifted Isabella's spirits, so it was in a cheerful atmosphere that they ordered their lobsters and salads and, after an enjoyable meal, headed to Candler Park, the affluent suburb where the Wests lived. Beverly took Isabella to her room then showed her the rest of the house. Just before they parted for the night, Isabella said,

'Beverly, do you mind if I tell you both about my problem with Yao tonight instead of tomorrow? I think I'll sleep better. '

'Not at all, honey, if you want to get it off your chest at once,' Beverly answered. 'I've never seen you looking so pinched – not even the year when you'd been sick. Change into something more comfortable while I go get Orlando.'

They sat in the basement. Orlando put on some soothing jazz then, looking as innocent as if they had no idea what was coming, he and Beverly waited for her to speak.

'Now, I don't know *where* to start…,' Isabella said, with an embarrassed laugh.

'At the beginning, honey.' Beverly said.' And don't worry about keeping us up. We're night owls and, in any case, we don't work Saturdays.'

'Alright… Yao and I grew up in very different churches. Mine, United Methodist, was much more informal than the Anglican church his family attended. Their sung liturgy and all those formal prayers have never done much for me; but it is Yao's church, and not getting much spiritual nourishment didn't matter until I got cancer. Sometime after my operation, I started becoming afraid that the cancer would come back, and that I wouldn't be so lucky the second time – more so when I was due for my check-ups. The oncologist kept assuring me that I was alright and unlikely to get it again, but the fear just got worse and worse. The only person I told about it was my best friend; I don't think you ever met her. She's called Ilara. I didn't tell Yao or Nanna because I didn't want them to start worrying and fussing over me when I knew they couldn't do anything to make the fear go away. And I didn't tell my doctor because he would have put me on tranquillisers. I didn't want that. So I just pretended everything was alright, and I did it very well because nobody ever suspected what was going on inside me. Not even Yao. I don't know how long I would have been able to keep it up, but last year, the twins joined a charismatic church near their campus. They told me about the experience and, from what they said, I began to think that a church like that might be what I needed…Again, I didn't discuss it with Yao because he got really, really mad when the twins told him they were born-again…The headquarters of their church is in Freetown, and I visited it with Nanna and Adora, but found all of them too young – even the pastor… Fast forward. Ilara told me about a Nigerian pastor who had started a ministry in Freetown and was supposed to have performed miracles through prayer, so I decided to investigate. Nanna came with me again, but I don't think she knew what I was really after…Orlando… Beverly… During the service, that pastor said he'd received a message from God about someone who needed healing, and he picked me out in the congregation. When I went forward, he prayed over me and, without asking what was wrong, ordered the fear tormenting me to leave… And it did. Just like that. I *felt* it leave me. After that experience, I felt I needed to stay close to him in case the fear came back, so I started going to the church every Sunday and to Bible study on Wednesday evenings. Yao was still upset about the twins, so you can imagine how he reacted when I, too, started going to a charismatic church. He hardly spoke to me, and he even supported Adora when she refused to listen to me about not wearing certain clothes; you know how immodestly the kids dress now…Fast forward again…The day before my dad was shot, Yao found a boy kissing Adora by the gate while I was at Bible study. According to Khadi, but for Nanna, he would have given Adora a good beating. We had a *big* fight about that, and he blamed me for neglecting my family and for destroying the peace and love in our home....'

Isabella's voice had become shaky as she described her healing. By the time she came to her quarrel with Yao, her lips were quivering so badly she had difficulty speaking. 'What has happened is mainly my fault, I know,' she lamented. 'Yao can't stand the way I dress now and the fact that I'm never home for lunch on Sundays or for our evening meal on Wednesdays.... And, he's very, very hurt that I kept how I was feeling from him...I want to put things right between us but, as far as Christianity is concerned, I *can't* go back to the way I used to be...I'm so confused.' By now she was weeping, and Beverly came over to comfort her, saying, 'Oh, honey.'

Orlando said, 'I'll be right back'; but he didn't return for a while which made Isabella think she must have embarrassed him. As her tears subsided, Beverly said,

'You know something, honey, I too almost joined a different church from the one Orlando and I belong to. Twenty years ago. He went off the rails for a bit and I left him.'

'Really! I *can't* imagine that.' Isabella joked as she dried her eyes. 'You both always seem so tight.'

'Most marriages go through some drama or other, honey,' Beverly said, laughing with her. 'If a couple really want to stay together, as I'm sure you and Yao do, they can usually work things out… Orlando and I were separated for nearly a year, but in the end I went back to him. '

'And to your original church?'

'Yes, but that had nothing to do with forgiving Orlando. By then I'd become more than a little disillusioned…Tell me something. Do you feel happy about this new church deep inside, or is it just that you feel obliged to keep going there because the pastor healed you?…Also, did you change your way of dressing because you genuinely wanted to be less glamorous, or was it because of something the pastor said, or because that was how everyone else in the church was dressing?'

'I enjoy most of the service much more than the Cathedral,' Isabella answered, 'but to tell you the truth, all that noise and drama and arm waving gets too much for me sometimes. And it's worse at Bible study. I am basically a private person so I get embarrassed the way one or two people carry on. And I don't like the way Pastor Hezekiah talks about other denominations and religions. He can be very judgmental, which I don't feel is right...I suppose my answer to the first question has to be that I'm not entirely happy. But he did heal me, of that I have no doubt... As for the clothes, it's not just that all the church members dress like that. It came up at Bible study; how women should dress modestly at all times and not wear men's clothing...'

'But, honey, modest doesn't have to be unattractive or boring,' Beverly said. 'Frankly, I'm with Yao on this, if the way you dressed to come here is how you look all the time now...It's depressing. I thought it was because you were in mourning...'

'I'm just trying to be a good Christian... 'Isabella said.

Just then, Orlando returned. He was rubbing his hands together as if something good had happened that he couldn't wait to tell them.

'Bella,' he said, 'while you were talking, I had an idea. That's why I left so suddenly; I went to find out if I could make it work. My idea is for you to have a talk with our former rector, Reverend John Parker. I had to check before I told you because, though he's retired, he still preaches and is often busy on Saturdays. He says he can fit you in between eleven and twelve...'

'Honey, that's *great!*' Beverly exclaimed, beaming at Orlando. Before Isabella could respond, she went on, 'Bella, you *must* go. John is an absolute sweetheart. *And* he's been caring for people's souls for a long, long time.'

'To talk to a perfect stranger about something so personal?' Isabella said.

'Sometimes it's easier to talk to a stranger, you know,' Orlando said. 'But, I promise you, after five minutes you'll forget that John is a stranger...Trust me.'

They knew Isabella was warming to the idea when she became interested enough to ask whether John Parker was black or white.

'He could pass for white,' Orlando said, 'But he's never tried to hide the fact that his great-grandparents were born into slavery – right here in Georgia...Have you by any chance read a famous book about our civil war called *Gone with the Wind?*'

'No, but I've seen the movie on satellite TV.'

'Do you remember that the story is set in Georgia?'

'Now that you mention it,' Isabella said. 'But isn't life interesting! Who would have thought that one day I would have family connections in the very place where that story was set?'

'You're right,' Orlando smiled, 'Who would have thought? Anyway, John's house is just like the one in *Gone with the Wind*, only less than half the size.

His wife passed five years ago; a housekeeper looks after him now.'

'Is she fat and slow like the nanny in the story?' Isabella asked with a chuckle.

'Just the opposite,' Orlando laughed. 'She's barely above five foot and moves around pretty fast...Bella, you'll like John, believe me, and I know from experience that he'll give you sound advice. Bev and I are too close to the two of you for that.'

Making up her mind, all of a sudden, Isabella said, 'Alright, I'll go. Thanks for arranging it for me.'

'Good; that's settled,' Beverly said. 'Now, off to bed, honey...Do you need something to help you sleep?'

'Falling asleep isn't usually a problem for me, thank God,' Isabella answered. 'But could I have a big glass of water, please?'

She hugged them both, suspecting that once she was out of hearing, she and Yao would be the topic of the Wests' conversation. They were indeed, but only as part of their nightly communion with God.

Breakfast the next morning was a heap of blueberry pancakes smothered in maple syrup, to be washed down with coffee, fruit juice, or both. Isabella had become careful of her diet since her cancer scare.

She opted for apple juice and took only one pancake, though they looked and tasted delicious.

'Nervous?' Orlando asked her as they set off in his luxurious black Lexus.

'A bit, but only because of the circumstances. Usually I enjoy meeting new people.'

'It'll be alright, you'll see.'

The housekeeper, Mrs. Washby, ushered them into a small, sunny, room with blue-green chintz curtains and easy chairs upholstered in the same fine fabric. Five minutes later, the Reverend Dr. John Parker appeared. He was a tall man, now slightly stooped, with wavy grey hair, and penetrating brown eyes slightly hooded by wrinkled eyelids. Isabella guessed his age to be in the late-seventies.

'Welcome to Atlanta, Isabella,' he said as they shook hands, 'May I call you that?'

His voice was such a soothing drawl that Isabella couldn't imagine it delivering a sermon, yet Reverend Parker exuded such authority and inner strength that she had no doubt that he would rise to the occasion.

'Of course!' she said, giving him her best smile.

'Good; and you may call me John. Orlando here is my small brother, so I consider you family, more so since I've met your charming mother-in-law.

197

I trust you left her well.'

'Yes, very well, thank you.'

At that point, Orlando excused himself, saying he would be back in an hour.

'I was so very sorry to hear about your father,' John Parker said, with a kindly glance, when they were alone. 'We have many problems in this country; guns in the wrong hands are among the worst.'

As Orlando had promised, Isabella soon felt as comfortable in his presence as if he were a favourite uncle, though she knew she would never bring herself to call him by his first name, not even after ten years working at *Health for the World* where she had grown quite used to American informality. As far as Reverend Parker was concerned, she couldn't forget the age and seniority proprieties instilled into her since childhood, though she hoped she'd be able to resist the urge to add a 'sir' when she answered him.

He led her to a book-lined study, sat her down opposite him at a desk of dark, highly polished wood, and bowed his head for a minute of silent prayer.

'Alright, honey, tell me your trouble,' he said, then stopped her before she could begin. 'No, before we go there... Orlando mentioned a few things on the phone, but I want to know more about you – only as much as you feel comfortable telling me, though.'

'We-ell... I'm forty-six years old, a college graduate – my subjects were English and economics. I am head of administration in the local office of a non-profit agency – an American one, as a matter of fact. It's called *Health for the World* and provides health care support in Sierra Leone, mainly to do with maternal and child health. I've been very happily married for twenty years. We have three children – twin boys, who are nineteen; they are at medical school at home, and we have a daughter who is fifteen. Three years ago, I got breast cancer. That is what led to the trouble...'

'Very concise,' Reverend Parker said with an admiring smile. '*Now* tell me all about it.'

Grateful that she was able to control her emotions on this occasion, Isabella repeated most of what she'd told the Wests. When she stopped speaking, John Parker said in his quiet way,

'I'm glad you now realise that you should have confided in your husband, Isabella. He has every right to feel offended on that score; you're going to have to eat a big slice of humble pie.'

'I've already started eating it,' Isabella told him. 'I asked his forgiveness before coming over here, and I don't mind doing it over and over again. The real problem is our conflict over my attending a charismatic church, and all that entails – long services, two-hour Bible classes every week, changes in the way I dress. Beverly and I talked about it last night. I told her that there are things about the church that make me uncomfortable, but that I feel I should stay close to the pastor who healed me. As far as my clothes are concerned, I'm only trying to be obedient. God has done such wonderful things for me. I feel it's the least I can do.'

'Alright, let's unpack. Your husband is a Christian?'

Isabella was quiet for a moment, then she said,

'If you'd asked me that even six months ago, I would have said yes at once. My husband loves his church and hardly ever misses a Sunday service. For the past year he's been one of the sidesmen – I don't know what you call them here – the people who assist the vicar; collecting and counting the offering and so on...'

'Ushers.'

'Yes, an usher. And he's been a loving, faithful husband, a responsible father, and a caring son. The reason, I now hesitate to say he's a Christian is because he's just too content with the way he is...'

'You mean, he doesn't seem to feel any need to grow spiritually.'

'Yes. It wasn't an issue before I started going to a charismatic church, but...'

'You shouldn't be making it an issue now. Until he himself feels the need for spiritual growth, behaving in a holier than thou, judgmental way will only put him off; as it has done already...Yes?'

'Yes,' Isabella admitted, with a rueful smile.

'So that's another thing you need to fix...Just keep on praying for him, and let him see how much *you* are growing in grace as a result of becoming a more committed Christian...He has to work out his own salvation, and for that to happen, *he* has to feel that he needs something more. From what you've told me, as far as behaviour is concerned, I would say he's pretty close to the kingdom...'

'Yes, he's a good person,' Isabella said.

'Only God is good, honey, but I know what you mean. Now, let's talk about your going to that particular church. Were you meant to remain with that pastor, you wouldn't be feeling uncomfortable about this, that and the other. You'd be feeling deep inner peace and contentment, as if you'd found your spiritual home. Your healing came through him, Isabella, but it was God who healed you. The Holy Spirit goes wherever it wants to, using people as it wants to. Perhaps that was all the pastor was supposed to do for you; not draw you permanently into his particular fold... '

'I hadn't thought of it that way,' Isabella murmured.

'Well, think about it now, and pray about it as well. The answer will come…And now, the clothes,' John Parker smiled. 'Tell me your honest feelings about clothes?'

'Well, they were not the focus of my life,' Isabella chuckled, 'but I liked being in fashion. And I liked it when my husband told me I looked pretty in a particular outfit…'

'Sounds like dressing the way you do now is an enormous sacrifice, and one you're only making because you think you should…'

'Yes, but I'm very willing to make it.'

'Would you say you used to dress immodestly or flashily?'

'My husband would have had something to say, if that were the case. He's quite conservative,' Isabella answered, laughing. 'But I did like high heels and interesting earrings and bracelets, and doing different things with my hair… And I liked lipstick…'

'All pretty harmless, I would say – even more so if your husband liked you that way, and you weren't doing it to attract other men, or to show off…'

'Oh, no!' Isabella said, shocked by the idea.

Thus far in their interview, John Parker had been sitting back in his chair in a relaxed fashion, but now he leaned forward with his arms on his desk, and his eyes and voice took on the kind of intensity Isabella imagined would be present when he was delivering a sermon.

'Listen, honey… What we call the Holy Bible is a collection of books, tracts, articles and letters, written by different individuals at different periods of history – a small library is what it is. Some of the books in it were even written by more than one person…Did you know that? Sure, the writers were men of God, for the most part, but no matter how devout or inspired they were, they were still human beings with opinions and prejudices and attitudes, based on their own mentalities and experiences, as well as the cultures and traditions they came from. We pastors, therefore, have a huge responsibility to avoid causing harm by treating the Bible as if God Himself dictated every word. That can be dangerously misleading, particularly if we cherry-pick passages to steer people in a particular direction. So… the first thing I want to say to you is this: apart from the words we believe were spoken by our Lord himself, most of the ideas sometimes taken as divine, are man-made, that is to say, they are human. Not that they have no value; many of them are of great help to folks on the spiritual path, but they shouldn't be put on the same level as divine commandments…And times change, you know. Even charismatic churches, which have come closest to preaching that every word in the Bible is infallible, have adopted some ideas and abandoned others. For example, women preach and give testimonies in church, and people speak in tongues during services, even though, according to the Bible, women are to be silent in church, and speaking in tongues, without interpreters, is to be strongly discouraged… It's often a matter of interpretation and emphasis, or what particular denominations seek to achieve. That's why there are so many of them.' This was clearly a topic close to John Parker's heart because, though his expression remained grave, after those forceful assertions, he sat back again and reverted to his soothing drawl. 'Isabella, Jesus condensed the ten commandments into just two: I assume you know what they are….'

'Yes, to love God with all my heart, and mind and soul and strength, and my neighbour as myself…'

'Good. The second thing I want to tell you is this: be guided by those two commandments in your thoughts, words and actions, and you won't go far wrong…You must have heard of St. Augustine…'

'Yes,' Isabella said.

'Well, St Augustine put it this way – perhaps you've heard the quotation before – "Love God and do as you please," meaning that when we love God and our fellow humans as He's commanded, we usually do the right thing...And you have a particular duty of love and comfort to your husband – remember that. He should be first among your neighbours.' He smiled into Isabella's eyes, 'From the way you spoke about him just now, I don't think that's a duty you find hard...'

'Not usually,' she laughed.

John Parker's smile grew even warmer.

'You'll be alright, honey; I have a good feeling...Now, I need a cold drink and I'm sure you do too...'

He picked up the handset of an internal phone and said into it,

'Odetta, please be good enough to bring us two glasses and a jug of that delicious lemony, minty thing you do – with plenty of ice. We'll be in the small living-room.'

They were enjoying their drinks and chatting pleasantly about other things, when Orlando rejoined them.

'Are you coming to hear me preach tomorrow?' John Parker asked when they were about to leave.

'Wish we could, John, but we don't want to wear Bella out. We're going to Peachtree City for lunch with Ronald and Wendy, and she flies back to D.C. in the evening.'

Smiling down at Isabella, John Parker looked genuinely regretful.

'*Much* too soon,' he said before asking them to join him in a word of prayer.

Isabella hugged him spontaneously as they said goodbye.

'I shall never forget you, Pastor Parker. Thank you from the bottom of my heart.'

'It was a pleasure, honey,' John Parker answered. 'Orlando, let me know what happens, you hear? Meanwhile, I'll keep you all in my prayers.'

In the car, Orlando turned to Isabella with a grin,

'What did I tell you?'

'You were right; he's a charming man. He made me see my mistakes without making me feel bad... And he gave me plenty to think about.'

'Not today, though,' Orlando answered. 'Suzanne and Michael are on their way. Bev's putting together a light lunch, and later on we'll go someplace else nice for dinner.'

The following evening, Orlando phoned Cobola after he and Beverly returned home from dropping Isabella off at the airport.

'Nanna, I think you and Yao are in for a pleasant surprise when Bella returns,' he said. 'She stopped wrapping her head before she went back to Washington.'

'Oh, I'm so glad to hear that!' Cobola exclaimed.

'Yes. I hope it's a sign of other good changes to come...' he said, and told her what had happened.

'We didn't have to dig at all. Bella came out with the story on her very first night with us. I arranged for her to spend an hour with John Parker...Remember him?'

'That fine vicar of yours?'

Orlando chuckled. 'The same one, though he's retired now. And, by the way, he thinks *you* are charming...I don't know what he said to Bella, but whatever it was, it seems to have made a difference already.'

'Thank God,' Cobola breathed. 'Thank you, my dear.'

'And Yao?'

' I think Bella, too, will have a pleasant surprise when she comes back. He came to his senses as we hoped he would, and not only that, he agreed for us to start having family prayers in the evening. He's even become comfortable about praying in front of us – heartfelt prayers.'

'So let's keep our fingers crossed,' Orlando said.

'And our prayers flying upwards.'

'That goes without saying, Nanna. Don't forget to keep us posted.'

# FOURTEEN

Knowing he would be meeting Isabella later that day, Yao wore the pale blue shirt she'd given him on his last birthday, and one of her favourites among his collection of neckties. It would have been more convenient to catch the ferry from Government Wharf, which was just down the road from his office, but since Isabella was travelling home via Accra and would arrive before four o'clock in the afternoon, he decided to use the Pelican water taxi to Lungi and back which would get them home faster. Having dismissed Sheku at lunchtime, he drove himself to the terminal beneath the Aberdeen Bridge.

He had half an hour to wait for the boarding call and spent much of it wondering how the rest of the day would unfold. In the two weeks Isabella had been away, they'd spoken to each other every other day, but their five-minute conversations had tacitly avoided any of their personal issues, dwelling instead on funeral arrangements, the funeral itself, and on inquiries about the well-being of family members in Freetown, Washington D.C and Atlanta. He'd decided that they needed to have a heart-to-heart, and the thought of it was making him as nervous as he'd been on his wedding day. The big difference, on this occasion, was that it occurred to him to pray for divine guidance before boarding the speedboat.

At the airport, an hour later, his heart thudded twice when the arrival of the Kenya Airways flight was announced. He allowed forty minutes for Isabella to disembark, go through immigration, claim her baggage and pass through customs, before taking a deep breath and positioning himself as close as he could to the entrance of the Arrivals Hall. He didn't have long to wait. Passengers coming from Accra were few that day, and no other flight had arrived. For the same reason, it was easy to spot Isabella.

A wave of relief surged through Yao, for though she was all in black and wearing flat shoes, she had on well fitting calf-length linen trousers which showed off the shapely legs and ankles that had attracted him years ago. Her cowl neck tunic top was sleeveless, and her head was bare, crowned by what he supposed to be the latest twists. He wanted to fold her in his arms there and then, but the large and laden trolley she was pushing prevented full body contact and besides, he was anxious to catch the first water taxi. So, after the briefest of kisses he hurried them through the would—be helpers milling around and, since he already had their tickets, on to the shuttle bus. Only when they were seated and waiting to be driven down to the jetty did he turn to her, showing his dimple,

'Welcome home, Babes.'

In her fragile emotional state, Isabella's eyes immediately filled with tears and, ignoring the other passengers, she put an arm around his neck and kissed him again.

'Yao…' she began, but he said, 'Babes, not now. You and I are going on a twenty-four hour retreat tomorrow. *Then* we'll talk, and I mean really talk.'

'But I want to see the boys,' Isabella said.

'You will see your sons,' Yao assured her. 'They promised to come home straight after their last class today and spend the night. We'll have breakfast early tomorrow morning, take them to where they can get transport for Kossoh Town, then go on to the Lighthouse Hotel until Sunday afternoon. No church. Okay?'

'Okay,' Isabella said meekly.

On the speedboat, he said, 'By the way, we have two new members of the family…Kobra and Kiki – guard dogs. Even *we* jump when they bark…'

'Guard dogs! Why now?'

'Well…, when you were away…Actually, it was the very night you left, armed robbers came to the house…'

Isabella stared at him in open-mouthed horror.

'Yes, armed robbers. Armed with knives. They followed me into the compound when I came from the airport. Area boys; they even knew my name. They stole our mobiles, all the money we had, except what Nanna had in her secret hiding places, my watch, Nanna's gold jewellery and some of your silver things. What hurt me the most was that they forced Nanna to give them her rings...'

'Ay, ya! How did she take it?'

'You know Nanna – philosophically; but she was shaken-o, so was Adora. So was I, for that matter, but we've got over it.'

'*Now* I understand why you were so strange,' Isabella said, remembering her confusion when she called home the day she arrived in Washington.

'We thought you had enough to deal with; that's why I didn't tell you then. We didn't even mention it to Orlando in case something slipped out.'

'Anyway, thank God it wasn't worse,' Isabella said.

'Yes. As you know, I don't trust watchmen, so I decided to get dogs instead. They cost an arm and a leg, but they are a male and a female. I'm thinking that we can sell their puppies and make some money.'

'Good idea...Kobra and Kiki...Who chose those names?' Isabella asked, with amusement.

'The people I bought them from – Boss Man's German friends. Kobra is the male. His name is spelt with a 'K' to match Kiki, who is the female; that's what is on their card for rabies shots. They are a mixture of a local mongrel and a Rottweiler, so they have long legs.'

'I love them already,' Isabella said. Her voice and glowing eyes embraced the entire family, but in particular, the person sitting beside her. 'What else?'

' Nanna says we have to start thinking about another helper for her because Ida is pregnant again. But there's time. She's not even showing yet.'

'Yes, plenty of time. What else?'

'That will have to wait till tomorrow,' Yao said, patting her knee.

'Enh.'

'Yes.'

'Okay.'

They lapsed into a thoughtful but relaxed silence, and when they spoke again, it was about trivial matters.

Gertrude phoned Cobola the next morning.

'How are things?'

'I don't know-o, my sister, but Bella is

looking better. And she has stopped wearing those depressing clothes and wrapping her head.'

'*Ehn*!'

'Yes. And they chatted nicely together while we were eating. They are not even here now. They've gone to a hotel to talk things over. Yao says they are switching off their mobiles for twenty-four hours, and that if there's any emergency we should call the hotel. He left the number.'

'*Enh*! Let's hope it will end up being a second honeymoon.'

'Yes-o. Let's hope; and pray.'

The next morning, it began to drizzle just as Yao and Isabella set off with the twins, and by the time they reached their *poda-poda* stop, the clouds had opened, releasing a torrent of water. Not having the heart to leave the boys in a downpour, Yao drove them all the way to Kossoh Town. Consequently, it was nearing two o'clock before they registered at the Lighthouse Hotel.

Since he hadn't reserved a suite, Yao expressed surprise when he saw that their accommodation was partitioned into sleeping and sitting areas. He went to inspect the bedroom with the porter while Isabella opened the curtains in the sitting room.

They concealed a glazed door which led to a balcony overlooking the Atlantic Ocean. The rain had finally ceased, but it was far too gloomy and damp for her to want to spend much time on the balcony and she went back inside, just as Yao turned away from the main door after the porter's departure.

'Hi,' they said with smiles and their gazes held, sparking desire neither had felt for quite a while. Its intensity propelled them straight to each other's arms and without a word, clutching each other, they stumbled into the next room.

'What are you laughing at?' Yao asked when his breathing returned to normal.

'At us.' In the urgency of passion, they'd ended up across the bed, only half undressed. 'If those people down at the reception saw us now, they would never believe we are really Mr. and Mrs....'

'It wasn't supposed to happen at all – at least, not now. My plan was that we'd talk, have lunch, talk some more, have dinner, talk some more, then *maybe*... Didn't you notice how I kept my distance last night?'

'I noticed. I, too, thought we'd have to settle our differences before anything else.'

'Obviously, I should have informed our bodies of the agenda,' Yao said drily.

'Obviously,' Isabella echoed.

As they chuckled over the unexpected turn of events, Yao said, 'I know exactly how Orlando would respond if I were to tell him this story...'

'Yes. "The best laid plans of mice and men..."' Isabella answered with an American accent.

That happy interlude ended when Yao glanced at his watch and saw that it was twenty to three. Rising with one swift movement, he pulled Isabella to her feet.

'Back to our programme. Let's go and eat before the restaurant closes.'

By the time they returned to their room, Isabella was feeling the effects of her long journey and emotional homecoming. She immediately undressed, lay on her stomach and hugged the pillow, hoping to sleep for a while. Yao, by contrast, was eager to press on with his agenda. He stripped to his boxer shorts and lay down beside her, but immediately said,

'So...Babes, why did you keep me in the dark when you had a problem?'

'Because of the problem,' Isabella mumbled.

'And what was it exactly? Nanna told me what she thought it was, but I want to hear it from you.'

With an audible sigh, Isabella turned to face him.

'I used to get very scared that the cancer would come back, Yao, and that I wouldn't be so lucky a second time. I thought that if I told you, you would make me go to the doctor and that *he* would put me on tranquillisers. I didn't want to become dependent on them. I kept hoping that as time went on the fear would go, but it became worse... I used to pray, but when the fear was really bad, I just couldn't focus on God the way Nanna had told me to... That was why I felt I had to go to another church...'

'You should have told me how you were feeling instead of pretending everything was alright. Even if you thought I couldn't help, you should have told me...'

'Yao, I know,' Isabella said with tearful contrition. 'Forgive me... Please. I beg.'

'Actually, I forgave you as soon as Nanna told me what she thought it was; but it hurt me-o, that you didn't tell me yourself – after all we'd been through together... It really hurt me.'

'It will never happen again. I promise.'

To her surprise, Yao said, 'Anyway, I, too, need forgiveness... Nanna made me see that...'

And so the long, healing conversation began. It continued for the rest of the day, interrupted only twice: when Yao had to let Isabella close her drooping eyelids, and when they went down to the restaurant for dinner. As soon as they returned to their room, they had showers and got into bed. That was when, sitting cross-legged, facing Yao who was again lying beside her, Isabella recounted her meeting with the Reverend John Parker.

'*He* was the one who finally put me straight,' she said, 'but Nanna and Beverly had also had their say.'

'In my own case, it was only Nanna. Do you know she heard us shouting at each other that night? She even heard some of the things we said to each other.'

' I know. I found out the day I left for the States – when I went to say goodbye. I was so ashamed.'

'Me, too; but not only about that. She and I talked at length the day after the robbery. She had told me before that instead of getting angry with you, I should take time to delve into why you were looking for another church so urgently, but I didn't listen to her. Had I taken her advice, I don't think we would have found ourselves in such a mess... She was right; I was thinking only about how *I* wanted my life to be...As a result of our talk, she suggested that we start having family prayers in the evenings.'

'And you agreed?'

'Mhm. Nanna, Adora and I have prayers every night now. Eight o'clock sharp, unless I have to go out. Adora and I take it in turns to read Bible passages that Nanna chooses. At first only Nanna prayed, but now she and I take it in turns.'

Isabella could hardly believe her ears.

'*You?*'

'I pray now-o, Babes,' Yao laughed. 'Even when I'm alone. Nanna is right; it helps.'

'You can't imagine how happy that makes me,' Isabella said.

'I don't want us to fight like that ever again. It was too painful. In fact, I have a suggestion about church...'

Instead of saying what it was, Yao suddenly raised himself on his elbow and stared with astonishment at Isabella who had, by now, stretched out beside him to relieve her aching knees.

'What?' she asked.

'Babes, I just realised something. That reverend in Atlanta mentioned St. Augustine to you, and Boss Man invited me to read the second lesson at their Rotary Club thanksgiving service last Sunday. Guess where they held it.'

'Not St. Augustine's.'

'*Yes!*'

'And that was the day after I spoke to Reverend Parker.'

'*Yes!...* It has to mean something.'

'I don't doubt that,' Isabella answered. 'After what happened to me, I'm open to any miracle, Yao. According to Reverend Parker, the Holy Spirit moves around, doing what it likes.'

'Anyway,' Yao said, subsiding, 'St Augustine's is both Anglican and interdenominational. They sang choruses as well as hymns during the service; the whole atmosphere was much more informal, *and*,' he added with emphasis, 'uplifting. I thought you could give it a try. If you like it, we can go there when I'm not on duty at the Cathedral...'

'Yao, I'll do anything for us to be together on Sundays like we used to be,' Isabella said, 'even go back to the Cathedral and suffer.'

'What about your Pastor Hezekiah?'

'He's not my Pastor Hezekiah, but even though Reverend Parker said it was God who healed me, not him, I'll always be grateful for the wonderful gift I got through him. I will give up the Bible study, especially now that we're having prayers at home but, if you don't mind, I'd like to go to his service sometimes – at least, for now...'

Yao wasn't entirely satisfied with that answer, but there'd been a sufficient meeting of their hearts and minds for him to give his consent and suggest that, since it wasn't that late, they get dressed again and go for a drink to new beginnings. However, that didn't happen. Isabella kissed him on the mouth, intending only to set a seal on their reconciliation before they went down to the bar; but one thing led to another and they lost all track of time till it was too late to do anything else but say a short prayer and sleep.

On Sunday evening, Cobola phoned Gertrude.

'Trudy,' she said, with glee, 'from the look of things, our prayers have been answered-o…You should have seen the two of them when they came in! Not at all like people with big children. Adora has been singing all over the place.'

'*Enh*! I wish I could have been a mosquito on the wall in their hotel room,' Gertrude said with one of her throaty chuckles.

'There you go again – busybody,' Cobola said in mock reproach.

'Cobs, stop pretending; you who are so romantic. I know you, too, would have liked to see how they got from A to B.'

'Mrs. Kargbo, that's enough! I'll see you on Wednesday morning. Good night.'

They ended their conversation chuckling.

221

# FIFTEEN

'I hope you people are not planning anything elaborate for my eightieth-o,' Cobola said to Yao and Isabella on a Saturday morning some weeks later. 'You've had *too* many unexpected expenses this year and besides, you know I don't like a crowd. '

Isabella answered, 'We haven't planned anything yet, Nanna, apart from deciding who will make your birthday cake.'

'In that case, let me tell you what *I* want, then you can plan accordingly. My birthday falls on a Sunday, so I want us all to go to Early Communion, including Auntie Gertrude. It's a pity Adora won't be confirmed till next year, but I want her to come along. Then, I want us to invite a few friends for lunch – like Manny and Hamida Martin and Ilara, our neighbours on either side, and so on. Not more than twenty people in all. We can hire canopies and have it right here in the compound. Sheku and Ida and Khadi will be on hand to help…And I don't want more than three short speeches, including mine. Yao, *you* make the main speech, since you know me better, and let Orlando propose the toast. *Short*-o. Then, I want Adora to sing something for me with one of her friends from Ballanta …'

'I hope it isn't that boy I saw kissing her.'

222

'And what if it is?' Cobola snapped. 'You know very well that his behaviour was quite normal, and that Adora is a sensible girl. Unless you have a better reason for objecting to him, I would like to hear them sing together.'

With Isabella giving him a warning look, Yao said,

'No objection, Nanna.'

'Good…Now about presents,' Cobola continued, ' I don't want any, but please let the guests know beforehand that if they were planning to give me anything, I would appreciate contributions towards helping Ida when she has to stop working for me. She has served me well, and I want to give her some money to start a small business that will allow her to care for her children at home. What do you think?'

'Nanna, that's a *great* idea,' Isabella said. 'Have you thought about what arrangement you'd like when she leaves?'

'To tell the truth, I don't like the thought of having to get used to a new person…'

'Then why don't we just get another general helper whom Khadi can supervise? During the day *you* will deal mainly with Khadi. She won't mind doing the personal things Ida does for you now, like massaging your feet. Adora will take over during the weekend and continue sleeping in the small room at night...'

'As long as the person is honest and irons well, *I* am fine with that,' Yao said.

Assuming that this domestic turn of the discussion held little interest for him, Cobola said,

'Alright, my dears. Let me not take up more of your time. Yao, are you playing tennis today?'

It was an innocent question, so she wondered why Isabella looked at Yao with raised eyebrows and twisted lips, and why Yao pretended not to notice and said that he might, but minding her own business, she didn't ask.

Since Yao continued to resist the idea of Adora being friends with a boy who wasn't a member of the family, and Adora had confirmed that Chimah felt shy about coming to their house after that unfortunate incident, Cobola decided to kill two birds with one stone. She invited Chimah to discuss what they would sing at her birthday lunch, planning to use the opportunity to introduce him to Yao and Isabella.

'Have you told Daddy and Mummy?' Adora asked.

'Of course, I have,' Cobola answered. 'They have no objection.'

The visit went well. Cobola took Chimah to Yao and Isabella herself to make the introduction. Yao was a little stiff at first, but when he discovered that Chimah's father was Athelstan Cummings, who had been two classes ahead of him in secondary school, and his House Captain, he reverted to his usual affable self, and even sent his regards to Chimah's parents.

They returned to Cobola's apartment where she settled them down with soft drinks and slices of cake, and poured herself a cup of tea.

'So…Have you thought about what you are going to sing?' she asked.

Before they could answer, she said, 'Let me tell you straightaway; for me words are important-o. And the tune shouldn't be boring.'

'Yes, Nanna,' Adora said.

Having missed this stage of life by becoming a wife and mother while still in her teens, Cobola enjoyed watching the young people confer in low voices, their heads close together. Finally, Adora said,

'Nanna, we want to do a gospel song. It's called *His eye is on the sparrow*, but I only remember the first verse…'

'Never mind, let me hear what you remember.'

Chimah's eyes radiated admiration as Adora sang,

*Why should I feel discouraged, why should the shadows come,*
*Why should my heart be lonely, and long for heaven and*
*home,*
*When Jesus is my portion? My constant friend is He.*
*His eye is on the sparrow and I know he watches me;*
*His eye is on the sparrow, and I know he watches me.*

*'I sing because I'm happy, I sing because I'm free;*
*For his eye is on the sparrow and I know he watches me.'*

'Darling, I *love* it,' Cobola said, moved already. 'Are you going to sing it in parts?'

'Only for the chorus, Nanna. Chimah is going to play his guitar as well.'

'*Hmm*! That will be *nice*. How many verses?'

'Three.'

'I'm sure everyone will enjoy it,' Cobola said. 'But where will you practice?'

'At Ballanta,' Chimah answered. 'We want our teacher to give us her opinion.'

'We want it to be *perfect*,' Adora said.

Cobola said she was sure it would be and thanked Chimah for coming. As he rose to take his leave, she said to Adora, 'Take him to say goodbye to Mummy and Daddy-o.'

Chimah and Adora exchanged glances, but they did as told before strolling to the gate where, conscious that Yao and Isabella were watching them from the veranda, they parted with decorum.

Later, Isabella said, 'Nanna, he seems like a nice boy. Very polite.'

'I thought so too. He's going to play his guitar at my birthday lunch, so I'm wondering if we shouldn't invite his parents.'

Expressing doubt, Isabella said, 'Let's ask Yao.'

Yao wasn't inclined to invite Chimah's parents, saying that might give the boy the impression that his friendship with Adora had received a seal of approval. Neither Cobola nor Isabella argued with him.

On Sunday, 28th November, 2010, her eightieth birthday, Cobola woke before six o'clock and, after her morning prayers, went for her shower which she could still take unaided, though she now sat on a plastic stool to do it. She had applied a moisturising lotion to her arms and legs, and was just thinking that she would like a cup of tea before church, when she heard a gentle knock on her bedroom door. It was Adora granting her wish, unasked. Right behind her came the twins, who were home for the weekend. They were carrying a gorgeous bouquet of pink anthurium and ferns, already in a vase, and presented it to her with a large birthday card which Beverly and Orlando had brought from the States. The Wests had arrived two days earlier and were staying at the posh Bintumani Hotel at Aberdeen, not far from Murray Town. On the outside of the card was a painting of yellow roses, and the words '80 Today!' in embossed gold lettering. Inside, were the names of every member of the immediate family, including Orlando, Beverly and their children.

'You all are so sweet!' Cobola said when she had read their individual messages and, with tears on her cheeks, hugged and kissed her grandchildren in turn. Yao and Isabella arrived a little later, already half dressed for church. This time it was *they* who hugged and kissed her.

'Nanna, do you need help with your dress?' Isabella asked.

'No, my dear. I can step into it,' Cobola said. 'I'll call Adora when I'm ready for the zip. What you can do is help me pin up my hair and put on my hat. This pain in my shoulders is making it hard for me to lift up my arms these days.'

That done, Isabella left her to continue the various other actions involved in getting dressed. Cobola took her time, taking sips of tea in between. The dress was a cream lace calf- length tunic, with a jacket, and matched the glamorous organza hat Beverly had sent her by Isabella. Cobola would have preferred something more modest, especially so early in the morning, but Isabella had firmly overruled her, saying, 'Nanna, reaching eighty is not a small achievement. This is your day.'

Cobola patted powder onto her cheeks, picked up her handbag and sat down to rest till, as previously arranged, Orlando and Beverly arrived in their hired car to convey her to the Cathedral. She had been disappointed, though not hurt, when Gertrude turned down the invitation to join them, saying her one experience of Cobola's 'aristo' church was more than enough for her.

'You'll find me at your house with breakfast ready, when you come,' she said. 'All the things you like: rice pap, rice *akara,* beans *akara*, with plenty of sauce, fried fish, stewed oysters, and plantains. There will be sausages, eggs, and baked beans for the Americans.'

As it turned out, only the twins ate the sausages, eggs and baked beans. The Americans, like everyone else, preferred the African food and stuffed themselves.

'Trudy, let's leave them to it, ya.' Cobola said after Orlando and Beverly had returned to their hotel to rest. The two women relaxed on Cobola's bed until two o'clock, then helped each other into their *bubus* – Gertrude's, the soft grey damask she had worn on her own eightieth birthday, which she had marked, but not celebrated because it fell just three months after Abu's death. Cobola's *bubu* was the same exquisitely embroidered lavender one she'd worn to Michael West's wedding.

Everything went according to plan. After a good, meaty, lunch, Kobra and Kiki were chained in the backyard, out of sight of visitors. Realising that no security duties were expected of them, they soon flopped to the ground and dozed the afternoon away. In the front of the house the setting was elegant, with white tablecloths under white canopies. Cobola sat at the high table with Gertrude, and a large round birthday cake, iced in white and lavender to match her gown. The inscription read: *Congratulations, Nanna, God bless you!* Cobola had wanted no candles; instead, an icing sugar '80', attached to a short white plastic skewer, completed the decoration of the cake. The food had been catered and was delicious, consisting of the usual festive fare of a large baked fish, a baked suckling pig, peppered chicken, Jolloff Rice, fried rice, all seasoned to perfection, as well as various salads.

The first item on the programme after lunch was Adora and Chimah performing *'His Eye is on the sparrow*' with a guitar accompaniment. Through their church contacts, the twins had provided a microphone and, as Adora had hoped, the rendition was perfect. She smiled at her grandmother afterwards and, dabbing her eyes, Cobola was the first to rise. In addition to joining in the standing ovation, she blew them kisses. Her pleasure increased when she saw Yao, who was next in line for the microphone, go up to Chimah, put a friendly arm around his shoulders and say a few words before giving Adora a peck on the cheek.

'Ladies and gentlemen, friends and family,' he said. 'I could talk for hours about this lovely woman, who happens to be my mother, but I've been instructed not to make a long speech, so I will obey orders and keep it short...' To applause, he went on, ' I don't think there is *anyone* who has had or has a mother as wonderful as mine, a mother who has always known when and how to lay down the law, when to fold me in her arms and comfort me, and who has loved me steadfastly and shown it even when I've been on my worst behaviour. I've appreciated her qualities even more since she came to live with us: appreciated her warmth, her wisdom, her unselfishness, her courage, her humanity, her prayerfulness, all of which have benefited the whole family and have been an inspiration to me. She would

231

be the first to tell you that she is far from perfect, but to us, she is the perfect mother, the perfect mother-in-law and the perfect grandmother. Nanna, my special prayer today is that we may have you with us for many, many more years. We all adore you.'

Long applause followed Yao's speech, which was just as well, because his voice had grown suspiciously husky as he neared the end of it. He had to clear his throat several times before he could speak clearly enough to ask Orlando to propose the toast to their mother. Orlando's speech was even shorter. With a fond glance at Cobola, he said,

'Nanna entered my own life very late, but since then, I've never stopped thanking the good Lord for the blessing of meeting her, and getting to know her. One thing Yao didn't mention is her sense of humour, and her ability to laugh at herself, which make her so much fun to be with. I echo Yao's prayer with my whole heart, and ask you all to raise your glasses and join me in drinking a toast to the health and happiness of a very special lady – Cobola Ennison – our Nanna.'

The cutting of the cake, and the singing of the birthday song followed, then it was Cobola's turn to speak. Taking her glass of water with her, she walked slowly up to the microphone which Derek was adjusting downwards to suit her height.

'Friends and family,' she began, 'I'm so glad I told my sons not to make long speeches because if they had said more, I don't think I would have been able to speak. Even now, it's hard.' She paused for a moment to compose herself before continuing. 'I've never been rich in terms of money, but when it comes to experiencing what life has to offer, I have been a millionaire. I have experienced the ugliness of life – poverty, people's unkindness, illness, danger and sorrow – deep, deep sorrow. But I have also experienced the beauty of life. So many blessings, so much joy, so much happiness...' Pointing to Gertrude, she said, 'This lady here, Mrs. Gertrude Kargbo, has been one special blessing – a faithful friend for more than sixty years.' She waited for the applause to die down before saying directly to Gertrude. 'Thank you, my dear sister, for the times you made me laugh when all I wanted to do was cry; and for all the tasty food you have used to fatten me over the years... Another big, big blessing has been the two children God gave me. Orlando and Yao, I love you both more than words can say. Thank you for making me feel so loved and *needed*... As for my grandchildren and great-grandchildren! How I wish I had them all by me all the time, but since that cannot be, I just thank God for them, and enjoy the three that are here as much as I can. Eric, Derek and Adora, you all give me a lot of joy, and keep me young at heart. God bless you, my darlings…Beverly and Isabella, my dear daughters-in-law. You are high on the list of my blessings. Thank you so much for making me welcome in your homes. And thank you for loving these sons of mine – in spite of their bald heads…' This last remark caused so much laughter that Cobola had time to take a few sips from her glass of water before going on. ' I mustn't forget our helpers, Khadi, Sheku and Ida. Each of them has been a blessing in one way or another – Ida in particular. She has looked after me well and also made me enjoy having another small baby to play with….When we were planning this lunch, we thought of letting one of my grandchildren give the vote of thanks, but I decided to do it myself because I truly appreciate you all giving up your Sunday rest to help me celebrate this day. Chimah Cummings. Please stand up, my dear…I want to say a special thank you to you for accompanying Adora when she sang for me just now. Your talent is going to give pleasure to many more people in the years ahead. I'm sure of that…Thank you all for coming and for making this special birthday so special. God bless you all.'

Cobola walked back to her seat, to lively applause and the singing of '*For she's a jolly good fellow*', pitched by one of their neighbours.

Not long after that, Gertrude said in a low voice, 'Cobs, I need my bed now-o.'

'And *I* need Maalox, otherwise I won't sleep tonight,' Cobola said. 'Let's go.'

She beckoned to Isabella, who was sitting nearby, sharing a joke with Ilara, and when she came up to their table, whispered in her ear,'

'You were right, my dear. Eighty is not a small age. Auntie Gertrude and I are feeling it. We are going. Please tell Orlando and Beverly I'll see them tomorrow. Thank you for everything…ya?"

Gertrude's empty dishes were loaded in the Volvo and Sheku drove her home. Having taken a spoonful of Maalox and her other medications, Cobola decided that she, too, would rest in bed. She couldn't lift her *bubu* over her head and so lay down just as she was.

The room was pitch black and all was quiet when, feeling the need to empty her bladder, she opened her eyes. She was still in her *bubu*, but someone had put down the mosquito net around her and covered her feet while she slept. She had a good idea which member of the family had been so thoughtful, but as she made her way to the bathroom, an uprush of love for them all made her murmur, 'Father, bless them and keep them. Let your face shine upon them, and be gracious unto them. Amen'

# EPILOGUE

Barely fourteen months later, Cobola Ennison supported Gertrude Kargbo's head as she took two sips of water and breathed her last, succumbing to pneumonia. As she closed her friend's eyes, Cobola said, 'Trudy, I'm right behind you.

And so it was. Even her family's constant love and attention couldn't make up for the loss of her lifelong companion and confidante. Cobola's health sharply declined, and she gradually lost interest in life outside her home. She stopped going to Early Communion on Wednesday mornings, settling instead for monthly home visits by one of the Anglican priests. She took no part in the 2012 general elections, which returned the same president and party, and always found some excuse when Yao invited her for a drive so she could see for herself how Wilkinson Road, and the area around it, had been transformed. The Wests visited Freetown after Gertrude Kargbo's death and, sadly observing his mother's deterioration, Orlando had known then that their next visit would be to attend her funeral.

Cobola Ennison died in her sleep in 2013, sometime after her usual affirmation that goodness and mercy would follow her all the days of her life – probably a massive stroke, her physician said, since her face showed no sign of struggle or pain. Having prayed that she would go quickly when her time came, Cobola would have been grateful for the way her life ended. And she departed in peace, knowing that all was well with her family. Yao had made the move to running his own business at the end of 2011, the year he turned fifty. He took over a petrol station whose previous owner, now elderly, had decided to give it up, and already had plans to add a convenience store to the premises. He was prospering in every aspect of his life, as were his wife and children in theirs. Orlando and Beverly West had retired from their medical practice and spent most of their time and a great deal of money travelling the world in cruise ships.

As Freetown funerals go, Cobola's wasn't a big one. She'd never been a public figure, and had been out of circulation as a midwife for more than two decades. She probably had relations on her mother's side in Guinea, but she'd never known them and, due to an old family feud, no relations on her father's side had featured in her life since his sister, her Auntie Aina, passed on. A good number of relations on her mother-in-law's side turned up, however, as did Yao and Isabella's friends; so did women Cobola had safely delivered of their babies over the years. Her sons read the lessons and, as had happened on her eightieth birthday, her twin grandsons, Eric and Derek, took up the elements for Holy Communion. Part of the Cathedral choir was on duty that day, but it was a quartet, made up of past students of the Ballanta Academy, that sang a lovely arrangement of *The Lord is my Shepherd,* Cobola's favourite psalm. 'It's by Franz Schubert,' Adora, Chimah, and the other two, told anyone who, having complimented them on their singing, wanted to know the name of the composer.

One year later, after attending the morning service at the Cathedral where, at Yao's request, Cobola Ennison had been mentioned, the immediate family, this time without the Wests, went to the Ascension Town Cemetery to unveil her tombstone. With so many years between their deaths, she had been buried in the same grave as her husband, Kweku, which would have delighted her tremendously, no doubt. Placed just below his, her tombstone reads:

**COBOLA ENNISON**
**'Our Nanna'**
**November 28 1930 – April 15 2013**
**Beloved mother and grandmother**
**†**
**Safe home, safe home**
**RIP**

239

www.ingramcontent.com/pod-product-compliance
Lightning Source LLC
Chambersburg PA
CBHW050726180626
46814CB00002B/625

\* 9 7 8 9 9 9 1 0 5 4 2 5 4 \*